A Wife in Name Only

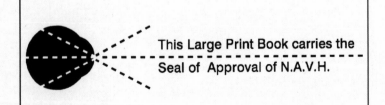

This Large Print Book carries the
Seal of Approval of N.A.V.H.

COLORADO CHRISTMAS, BOOK 3

A WIFE IN NAME ONLY

ROSEY DOW

THORNDIKE PRESS
A part of Gale, Cengage Learning

GALE
CENGAGE Learning™

Detroit • New York • San Francisco • New Haven, Conn • Waterville, Maine • London

GALE
CENGAGE Learning™

© 2007 by Rosey Dow.

All scripture quotations are taken from the King James Version of the Bible.

Thorndike Press, a part of Gale, Cengage Learning.

Thorndike Press® Large Print Christian Fiction.

The text of this Large Print edition is unabridged.

Other aspects of the book may vary from the original edition.

Set in 16 pt. Plantin.

LIBRARY OF CONGRESS CATALOGING-IN-PUBLICATION DATA

Dow, Rosey.
   A wife in name only : love comes in an unexpected package during the 1880s / by Rosey Dow. — Large print ed.
     p. cm. — (Colorado Christmas; bk. 3) (Thorndike Press large print Christian fiction)
   ISBN-13: 978-1-4104-3099-1 (hardcover)
   ISBN-10: 1-4104-3099-5 (hardcover)
   1. Colorado—History—1876–1950—Fiction. 2. Christmas stories. 3. Large type books. I. Title.
PS3554.O89W54 2010
813'.54—dc22   2010034515

Published in 2010 by arrangement with Barbour Publishing, Inc.

Printed in Mexico
1 2 3 4 5 6 7 14 13 12 11 10

To my dear friends at the
Calvary Baptist Church ladies
Bible study. You enrich my life.

CHAPTER 1

Colorado, October 1884

The sky over the mountains was dark and lowering when Katherine Priestly and her brother, Johnny, left their ranch to head south. Traveling on horseback in late October was always risky business in Colorado, and the sky wasn't making any promises. Huddling deep into the shawl wrapped around her head and shoulders, Katie squeezed her eyes shut. The last thing she needed was to add frozen tears to her misery.

The night before, she and Johnny had made their decision to leave home. It had been so hard leaving Ma and the four younger kids behind with just a little cornmeal and some flour in the larder and a small deer hanging in the smokehouse. It had been hard hugging them all good-bye and hearing their sniffles, especially Ma's. But facing the bitter wind and the steely sky were hardest of all.

They had to make it to Musgrove, the mining camp twenty miles southeast of their ranch. It was the only place they could think of to find work, a tiny spark of hope because this time of year the camps were almost shut down. Everyone with any sense headed home for the winter — except those desperate enough to stay there . . . or desperate enough to go there.

Doggedly heading into the wind, the Priestly siblings qualified in that respect. They were desperate enough to do anything that would feed their family through the frigid months ahead.

Their ranch had never been prosperous, but Pa had eked out enough to feed his six children and keep them in shoes. Until last August when anthrax had wiped out their herd. Within days, they were penniless and living on what Pa could shoot and Ma could scratch out of the ground in her kitchen garden.

When fall days shortened and the icy wind swept through, Pa gathered the children around. With Ma close to his side, he said, "I'm leaving in the morning to take a job with the railroad. It only pays twenty-five dollars a month, but with God's help it will feed us through the winter." He looked at

Johnny. "You'll have to take care of them for me, son."

He squeezed his wife's hand. "I'll be back come spring."

That was six weeks ago, and they hadn't heard from him since. Had he met with an accident? Had the railroad refused him work?

These questions gnawed at Katie's mind as the terrain grew rugged and the road all but disappeared. "How much further?" she called to Johnny ahead of her.

He pulled his horse up and waited for her to come up to him. "What was that, sis?" he asked. His sandy brown hair blew across his eyes. The top of his nose was red above the scarf covering the lower part of his face.

"How much longer?" she asked. "My feet are numb."

"We'd best find some shelter and build a fire," he said, scanning the area for a hollow or an offset in the rocky terrain. "There's a place." He urged his horse forward.

Half an hour later, they sipped weak coffee and held their feet toward the flickering fire.

"They hurt," Katie whispered, gazing at her boots.

"Don't take them off, sis," Johnny said. "You'll never get them back on." He glanced at the sky. "We can't stay here too much longer. What if it starts to snow?" He took a closer look at his sister's pinched face and drew her into his arms. "Here. Let's try to keep each other warm. That's what Pa and I did when we were out in that blizzard that time. We huddled up and waited it out."

Katie pulled her shawl higher until it completely covered her face. She pressed her cheek into Johnny's coat and tried to stop shivering. Johnny was a good brother. A year older than she, he'd always looked out for her.

All too soon, they were back in the saddle. The wind had died down a little. Now and then the sun tried a peek at the landscape.

When they rode into Musgrove, it was suppertime. The streets were clear. Not a person, a horse, or a wagon in sight. Katie was so cold and so exhausted, she could hardly stay in the saddle.

Johnny led the way to the hitching rail at the general store, a shanty with board walls and tent canvas for the roof. He helped Katie down, kept his arm around her, and supported her inside.

The warmth of the store almost felt painful to Katie's frozen cheeks. A potbelly stove glowed in the center of the room, and a slim, white-haired woman sat close by it in a rocking chair. When she saw them, she stood.

"Bring her here by the fire," she said, reaching for Katie's arm. "Where did you kids come from? You can't be from around here, and it's much too cold to be traveling."

Katie sank into the chair. It felt like a tiny spot of heaven. Her eyes drifted closed.

She heard Johnny say, "We rode down from our ranch, about twenty miles from here. We had to stop twice to thaw out . . ."

The rocking chair was soft with padding on the back and the seat. It wrapped around Katie's cold form while the heat from the fire seeped into her weary, aching muscles. Her head relaxed on the back of the chair, and she soon fell asleep.

"Katie!" Johnny's voice brought her out of the delicious warm stupor. She blinked and pushed away his hand.

"Here's some hot tea for you," he said, his voice insistent. "Drink it, sis. You need it."

She tried to focus on his face. The smell of the sweet tea caught her attention. "Thank you," she said, sitting up straighter and reaching for the blue enamel mug. She hadn't eaten anything since cornmeal gruel for breakfast.

"You'll stay for supper, of course," the storeowner said. "It's not much, but it's hot."

"We're obliged," Johnny said. He had his hat and coat off and was standing near Katie with his hands out to the stove. "My sister was all tuckered out."

Katie sipped the tea and savored the warmth traveling through her. "Did you ask about work?" she asked Johnny.

"Mrs. Sanford is going to hire me for the winter," he said. "Room, board, and five dollars a month."

"There aren't many customers this time of year," the storekeeper said. Her face was drawn and she had a hollow-eyed look. "But I can use someone to keep the snow shoveled away from the door and carry wood for me. Come spring, I want to start building a real store with a tin roof and windows in it. He can help with that, too, if he's a mind." She nodded, pleased.

"Five dollars?" Katie murmured. Even in these hard times, it was a meager amount.

Johnny knelt by her and whispered, "It's the best we can do, sis. No one else is hiring here. At least Ma won't have to feed me along with the others. I'll send the five dollars to her like clockwork."

She touched his chin, still soft as a child's

though he was nearly twenty. "What about me?" she asked, speaking louder and looking at Mrs. Sanford. "I need work, too."

Setting three bowls on a rough-hewn table nearby, the older woman looked up and shook her head. "There's nary a place hiring this time of year, girlie," she said. "I wish there was." Suddenly her gray eyebrows drew together. "Wait a minute. Wait a minute. There was someone in here . . ." She bent her head low, drumming her fingertips on the tabletop. Suddenly, she straightened, her finger pointed toward the canvas ceiling. "Masten! Brett Masten needs a cook at his ranch. He stopped in last month to see if anyone was pulling out of Musgrove and needing work."

"How far is that from here?" Johnny asked.

"Ten miles west," she replied. She looked at Katie. "You're not going anywhere tonight," she announced. "It don't cost nothing to loan a body a cot and a blanket now and then. You'll sleep here and head over there in the morning."

Katie nodded. "Thank you, Mrs. Sanford," she said, and she meant it.

Johnny got up to help Mrs. Sanford, and Katie finished her tea while she waited. What if the rancher had already found someone? What then?

Near noon the next day, Katie rode into the Masten ranch alone. It had been a nerve-wracking two hours, alone in the saddle, cold and scared, watching the landmarks and praying that Mrs. Sanford had been accurate in her directions. Katie wanted nothing more than to find a place, any place to roll up her sleeves and work. Preferably some place with a roaring fire, but any place would do.

The entrance to the ranch was marked by two tall posts with an arched piece of iron over the lane. It had the word "Masten" welded into it and a six-pointed star on each side.

The ranch yard was bare, free of trash but also free of any decoration. The bare wood of the buildings was gray and weathered, strong and sensible, with a long rambling cabin to the left of the lane and the barn door facing her straight ahead as she rode in.

She scanned the area, looking for someone to talk to. The cabin had two front doors, one at the closer end and one in the center. She had no idea which place to knock or where to put her horse. She also feared she'd fall if she tried to dismount alone. She'd stopped feeling her feet half an hour ago.

She brought her horse to a halt in front of the ranch house when a tall man stepped out of the barn. He paused in the doorway, his bushy white eyebrows raised in surprise. Rubbing his nose, he came toward her in a kind of sideways gait unique to old cowboys. He wore a stained Montana Stetson that had long ago lost its shape and was now only a rounded dome with a floppy brim.

"Help you, ma'am?" he asked. His voice was creaky and higher toned than Katie had expected. He had a round face and blue-gray eyes.

"I've c-come to see about a j-job," she stammered, partly from cold and partly from stark terror. What if Masten turned her down?

The cowboy turned toward the house. "The boss is inside, rustling up something for dinner, I reckon. He'll be mighty glad to see you." He pointed to the door in the center of the long building. "That's the kitchen door. Go on in."

She tried to kick her boot free of the stirrup, but it wouldn't come loose.

Without any fuss, he pushed the toe of her boot through the metal arch and offered

15

her his hands.

She gladly leaned on his strength and eased to the ground. Schooling herself to walk a straight line with those two frozen stumps she called feet, she headed toward the second set of steps and made it to the door. Knocking, she waited, willing her breathing to stay silent and slow.

"It's open!" a man's voice called.

She pushed and the wooden door moved inward. Feeling the warmth meeting her, she quickly entered and shut out the cold behind her.

After the wonderful heated air, the first thing she noticed was the smell. It was a mixture of charcoaled bacon and stale beans with a background aroma of fresh coffee. A lanky man bent over the stove, his left side facing her. He wore a blackened apron over jeans and a red-and-white checked shirt, his sleeves rolled to the elbows.

Behind him, a small square worktable was piled high with vegetable peels and dirty cooking pots. The table had soiled dishes stacked in the center where someone had simply moved the dirty dishes inward and set the table with clean ones — which were now dirty, too.

For a full minute Katie stood without moving, trying to decide whether to be pleased or disgusted. If this was the boss, he hadn't found a cook yet. On the other hand, what she was looking at would take two days of hard work to set to rights, besides the cooking she'd have to do as well.

"I'm here about a job," she faltered at last. "Mrs. Sanford at the general store in Musgrove . . ."

"Can you cook?" he demanded, looking at her for the first time. His voice was strident with an edge of desperation.

"Yes, sir."

"How old are you?" he asked, a little softer.

"Eighteen," she said, lifting her chin.

He pushed the smoking skillet away from the hot spot on the Franklin cook stove and picked up a grimy towel. "What brings you here, if I may ask?" he cocked his head a little, squinting one eye as he sized her up.

She licked her lips. Her feet were beginning to ache as they warmed up. "We lost our cattle to anthrax. I'm trying to find work to get through the winter."

He nodded. "That anthrax outbreak scared me spitless. We were spared, thank the Good Lord."

He pulled a chair away from the worktable. "Here. Sit down. We need to talk." When they were seated, he went on. "I'll

17

pay you thirty dollars a month. You can sleep in the room off the kitchen. It's back there." He nodded toward the hall that went off from the back of the room beyond the stove. "And you'll get your meals, of course."

She swallowed. "I'd like forty dollars," she said. "I have to send money home to Ma."

His eyes narrowed. He studied her, working his mouth outward. "There's one more thing we have to get settled. I have a rule here at the Masten Ranch. Once burnt, twice shy, as they say. I only hire married women. A single woman on a ranch full of single cowhands is a recipe for big trouble. As much as I need kitchen help, you'd end up being more of a problem than I can even describe if I don't enforce that rule."

Katie gulped. She felt the safe, comfortable warmth of that filthy kitchen slipping from her frantic grasp.

"That's all right then," she said, her voice tight. "I'm married."

CHAPTER 2

She cleared her throat and plunged ahead. "My husband just got a job with Mrs. Sanford at the general store in Musgrove. He sent me here since there was no work for me there. The town is all but closed down."

Still watching her closely, Masten slowly nodded. "I reckon we have a deal then," he drawled. "I'll have Duffy bring in your things."

"There's just a saddlebag," she said.

He pointed toward the stove. "Throw out that mess in the skillet," he said. "It's not fit to eat. We'll skip dinner today and wait for supper. The men won't mind one bit, believe me. I've been fighting a mutiny around here for six weeks. Not one of them will lift a finger to do 'women's work,' and I'm no account in the kitchen. Never was and never claimed to be."

"What happened to your cook?" she asked, untying her wool bonnet. Strands of her dark wavy hair fell around her face. She smoothed them back.

"He caught pneumonia. We did everything we could for him, poor hombre, but with no doctor and no medicine . . ." He sighed. "I'm mighty glad to see you, Mrs . . ."

"Priestly," she said. "Please call me Katie."

"I'm Brett," he said, smiling a little. He stood and found his ten-gallon hat. "I'll go out and spread the good news." Lifting a long buffalo coat from a peg, he whipped it on and stepped outside.

Pulling at the buttons on her black coat, Katie slowly made her way toward her room. Past the stove, a door opened off the tiny back hallway. She turned the knob and went inside. The room was medium sized with a narrow bedstead, a nightstand, and a small chest of drawers under the only window. At least the bed had a warm quilt on it. She laid her coat across the end of the bed and placed her bonnet on top of it.

She moved closer to look out the bare window into the back yard. How could she dress in here with a grand view of her entire room readily available to anyone who had a hankering to use the outhouse?

The same old cowhand appeared in her doorway. He was holding her saddlebags. "Here you are, ma'am," he said, bobbing his head.

"Thank you . . . Duffy, is it?" she asked, taking them from him.

"That's me all right."

"I'm Katie," she said. "Duffy, I'll need a bucket, a broom, and a mop. Can you find those for me?"

"Gladly," he said with a loose grin. "The hands are powerful glad to see you, Miss Katie. I guarantee they are."

"Just Katie," she said, trying out a timid smile. "No Miss."

His head bobbed again. "Suit yourself," he said. He turned away. "I'll rustle up a bucket and them other things for you." He disappeared toward the back door, and she heard him go outside.

Rolling up her sleeves, Katie set to work. Adding wood to the cook stove, she set on a pot of water to heat and started scraping plates. She'd never have the kitchen cleaned before suppertime, but she had to clean enough to begin to cook a meal. What had those males been doing? Re-using dirty pots? It was disgusting to even think about it.

Piling the first dishpan full of cups coated with dried coffee, she left them to soak while she put on a second pot of hot water. At this rate she'd have to take a break from cleaning to split some wood.

The kitchen was a wide room spanning about thirty feet. At Katie's right, a long work counter had a pitcher pump at the end nearest the door and cabinets beneath it. A window over the counter gave a broad view of the front yard. At the far end of the counter was a door on the south wall. She opened it and found that it led to a sitting room with a stone fireplace. After a quick peek, she closed the door.

The cook stove sat a few feet from the sitting-room door with a wood box nearby. The back hall opened up beyond the stove.

To Katie's left, a second window faced the front yard. She opened the side door on the north wall to see a row of six cots along the wall in front of her. On the other side of the room stood a potbelly stove and a small table with four chairs around it. Feeling like an intruder, Katie quickly closed that door, too.

A dining table and ten chairs filled the north end of the kitchen, and the back wall held a long bank of built-in cabinets. Every level surface was covered with dirty pans and dishes, many of them moldy. She found an apron and tied it on, ignoring the dark stains on it. She had to start somewhere.

Three hours later, Katie stepped out to

the stoop to jangle the triangle. It was just past four o'clock, early for supper but mighty late for dinner.

Within seconds, five men appeared in the barn door and aimed for the house like they had a purpose. Katie stayed on the stoop just long enough to get a look at them.

Besides Duffy and Brett Masten came a big bruiser of a man with wiry blond hair and a big, bulbous nose. He had a slow walk and an easy way of moving his shoulders, like a sleepy bear.

After them marched two younger men, one of them no more than five feet three inches tall, the other about five eight. The short man had wavy red hair and moved like he had springs in his shoes. The other one might have been Hispanic. He was about the same age as her brother Johnny. He was as dark as Johnny was fair and by far the handsomest of the cowhands.

Katie moved inside to set the food on the table while the men milled around the pump and basin, washing up.

"Boy, don't that smell good!" the bruiser said.

Red made a moaning noise. "My stomach thinks my mouth's sewed shut!"

Katie smiled at their enthusiasm. Biscuits and chipped-beef gravy wasn't exactly fancy cooking, but there was plenty of it. And it was good. She'd fixed herself a plate earlier. If there were leftovers, she was going to have a second helping and not feel guilty.

The men gathered around the table and waited while Brett bowed and thanked the Lord for the food. Then they dug in.

Ten minutes later, Katie refilled the serving dishes and wondered if there would be leftovers.

When the men were about finished with the meal, Brett held up his hand to silence their chatter. "Men, I'd like to introduce the lady who rode in today and saved our lives." He held his hand toward Katie.

Standing beside the kitchen's pump, she felt her face glowing.

Red gave a hoot and said, "Welcome home, ma'am!"

Brett said, "That's Rollie Barker."

The bruiser called out, "Yeah, his bark is worse than his bite."

Someone shoved the man's shoulder, and the rest laughed.

Brett laughed, too. "The one with the smart mouth down there is Lew Mullholland and beside him is Duffy Reed, our local weather man. And this," he clapped the Hispanic-looking guy on the back, "is Henry Hadley."

"Enrique!" Red called out, clapping.

The man in question endured the attention with a look of long-suffering. "Call me Hank," he said, speaking to Katie directly.

Red went on. "You'll have to forgive him. He's from Texas." He laughed at his own joke.

Brett said, "Everybody, this is Mrs. Katie Priestly, sent by the Good Lord to save us from starving."

From poisoning, more like it, Katie thought. She smiled. "Please call me Katie. Not Miss Katie, just Katie."

She got some salutes and a couple of nods.

"Great cooking!" Duffy said, reaching for yet another biscuit.

"The best!" Lew agreed, sopping up the gravy on his plate with a scrap of biscuit.

"I'll try to do better tomorrow," Katie said, apologetic. "There wasn't much time today."

Duffy chortled. "If it gets much better than this, my tongue'll beat my brains out."

The talk moved to ranching matters, and Katie turned her attention to cleaning up the pans from that meal and then moved to working on the dirty piles stacked on the counter.

She was drying a thick meat platter when the last of the hands drifted out. Brett Masten was still at the table. When the door banged closed, he stood. "Katie, you're welcome to sit at the table with us," he said, pulling his coat from its peg. "I didn't say anything just now because I didn't want to embarrass you if you'd rather not. The men are kind of rough . . ."

Her hand stopped wiping the platter. "That's kind of you, Mr. Masten." She hadn't expected this.

"Brett," he said with that small smile. He put on his ten-gallon hat. "You don't have to give me an answer or anything. If you want to, you can set yourself a place next time, that's all." He tipped his hat to her and headed out.

Katie set the platter on the far end of the counter where the clean dishes were stacked. She let out a small sigh of relief. This wasn't going to be so bad after all.

With a lighter heart and renewed energy, she cleared the table and quickly washed up the dishes from that meal. Washing up right away was so much easier than waiting until the food had turned to stone.

She opened every cabinet door along the back wall — five above the thick oak counter and five below it. Her mother had never enjoyed this much storage space. It was pure luxury. But the contents were a total shambles — food containers beside pottery dishes, pots piled with silverware.

Darkness fell, and Katie lit a lamp. Although she couldn't wash dishes by lamplight, she could surely empty those cabinets and start organizing.

Sometime later, the door on the south side of the kitchen opened and Brett stepped in, concern on his face. "Are you still at it?" he asked. "It's nigh on eight o'clock."

She set down the sack of rice she was holding. "I was hoping to set this to rights before I retire," she said. "It's so much easier to cook when things are in order."

His keen eyes seemed to look right through her. "All that stuff will still be there tomorrow. You rode in from Musgrove this morning, remember?" He made a shooing motion with both hands. "Please, go and rest. I didn't hire you to do everything in the first twelve hours."

She wiped her hands on her apron. "I suppose I should," she said. Her shoulders were aching. She felt them now. "But there is one thing." She hesitated, feeling a flush climbing her neck.

He waited for her to go on.

"I need a curtain for the window in my room," she said.

"A curtain?" He pulled in his chin as

27

though uncertain of her meaning.

"To cover the window . . . for privacy." Her face was flaming. Did she have to spell everything out to him?

His mouth opened a little as he slowly nodded. "Oh, yes. That." He seemed puzzled. "I'm afraid curtains are something I've never worried about up to now." His gaze wandered over the kitchen. "I wonder what we could use . . ."

"A sheet? A tablecloth?" she asked, hopefully.

He shook his head.

"A quilt," she went on, a little frantic now.

"A quilt! Yes, I have an extra one of those." His hand went to the doorknob behind him. "Let me see . . ." He disappeared into the shadows beyond the door.

Katie followed him, hesitant to enter his domain. Standing in the doorway, she took in a massive room, at least thirty feet long and fifteen feet wide. To the left was a stone fireplace that covered almost half of that tremendous length.

The room was practically bare. Four wooden chairs sat in a half-circle around the firebox that glowed orange from a large bank of embers. The floors had no rugs. The three mullioned windows gave her a cold, black stare.

Brett lit a lamp and moved through one of the two doors on that long back wall. He returned in a moment with a tattered blanket over his arm and held it out to her. "This is the best I can do, I'm afraid," he said. He looked sheepish. "Since that bad experience with that *single* female cook ten years ago, I haven't had a woman on the place. No womenfolk at all. I'm afraid things are a little rough."

"Thank you," she said, taking the blanket. She turned back to the kitchen. "Good night." She softly closed the door after herself. A little rough indeed.

She found a couple of tacks in a tin can that had been shoved back into a cabinet. Using the heel of her shoe, she held the center of the quilt's edge in her teeth and pounded in three tacks. Miracle of miracles, it held.

The room felt like an icehouse. She made a mental note to leave her door open in the evenings from now on to warm it up before she went to bed. She didn't feel secure leaving the door open while she was sleeping, so she laid her coat over the quilt and tried to ignore her cold toes. Spring seemed a hundred years away.

When Katie woke up, her knees were touching her chin, and the quilt was over her head. What was it? Some kind of a noise that woke her? She peeked out of the covers. The room was dark. Another noise. Someone at the woodpile outside the back door was stacking logs.

It must be morning. Scratching around in the darkness, she found a match and scraped it against the bedpost. Shivering, she lit the lamp and hurried into her clothes. She was fastening the buttons on her shoes when heavy boots passed her door. The wood box rumbled with the sound of dropping sticks.

She combed her dark hair and pulled it back into its usual high ponytail. She'd been blessed with natural waves, but that made it hard to catch all the strands at one swipe.

Finally, she was ready. She picked up the lantern.

When she stepped into the kitchen, Brett was squatting before the cook stove, holding a match inside its front door. "Morning," he said, barely glancing at her. "Fire went out. I forgot to stoke it last night." He peered inside the stove and carefully added a sliver of kindling.

"You mean I forgot," she said. "I'm sorry. It won't happen again."

He kept his gaze on the tiny flames.

"Don't worry about it. I should have mentioned it. It was completely my fault."

She went to the pitcher pump and filled the washbasin. Patting ice-cold water onto her face, she reached for the hand towel hanging beside the pump. "How about eggs?" she asked, turning to face him. "Do you have chickens?"

He nodded. "We keep the eggs in a box in the henhouse this time of year to keep them cold. Whenever you need any, ask one of the boys and he'll fetch them for you. I'll have Rollie bring some in now."

"That won't be necessary," she retorted. "I can fetch them just fine."

His eyebrows raised a fraction of an inch. He added a small log to the fire. "The chicken house is out the back door and to the right about a hundred feet. It's up against the corral fence. You can't miss it. Just follow your nose."

She looked at him to see if he'd meant that as a joke, but his face was as calm and serene as ever. "What time do you usually have breakfast?" she asked him.

"Six o'clock or thereabouts," he said, clanging the door closed. Dusting his hands, he unfolded his legs like a lady opening a fan and stood up.

Watching his face, Katie's head bent back

further and further. He was at least a full foot taller than she. Why hadn't she noticed it until now? She stepped away to ease her embarrassment. "We'll have hotcakes and sorghum for breakfast, if that's all right," she said.

"Katie, if you fixed scrambled wagon tracks and fried cow chips, the boys would think it's just fine," he told her with a small smile. He looked around. "Is there anything else you need before I see to the chores?"

"I'm perfectly fine," she said. "We may be a few minutes late this morning, but I'll call when I'm ready."

"Jangle the triangle on the stoop, and they'll come a-running." He lifted his buffalo coat from the wall and gave her a nod. Then he went out.

Setting the coffeepot on to brew, she got busy. At fifteen past six, she called the hands in. This time she sat with them, at a corner far from Brett at the head of the table and with one empty chair between herself and Rollie.

"Hot cakes!" Duffy exclaimed, eyeing the tall stack of golden discs. "I haven't eaten hotcakes in nigh on five years."

Rollie turned to Katie. "Old Cappy didn't cook anything but bacon and biscuits for breakfast."

Lew added, "Once in a blue moon he'd work himself up to a pan of sweet rolls."

"Every other Christmas or so," Duffy added.

"Let's pray," Brett said, and all bowed their heads.

A few minutes later, Rollie leaned a little toward Katie. "So, where are you from?" he asked.

"We have a ranch a little west of Muddy Creek," she said, reluctantly.

"You still have it?" Lew asked.

She nodded, her eyes on her fork as it cut a piece of bacon. "We got hit with anthrax last summer."

A heavy silence settled around them. "Too bad," Duffy said. He glanced at Brett. "But for the Good Lord . . ."

"There goes us," Brett finished. "At least a dozen ranchers were wiped out. Others lost everything, but they're too stubborn to call it quits."

"I guess we fall into the second category," Katie said, trying to smile. She had a sudden image of her five-year-old sister, Arlene, hugging her arms tight across her hungry stomach and crying. Suddenly, Katie's breakfast tasted dry.

"Anyone want more coffee?" she asked, getting up to fetch the pot.

Brett began to discuss the business of the day, and the mood was broken. For the men, at least.

After they left the kitchen, Katie's tears dripped onto her shirtwaist. If only she had money to send her family now.

That evening after supper, the hands headed through that door on the north wall.

A few minutes later, Brett came into the kitchen and sat at the table with his account books. Katie was rinsing pinto beans. She planned to start them soaking before she retired.

"Tomorrow I'll make a passel of bread," she said. "I finished cleaning out the cabinets this afternoon."

He gazed around the room. "It looks like a new place," he said warmly. "You've done better than I ever imagined. The boys like you, too." He smiled at her, then wrote something in his ledger.

"Mr. Masten," she said, closing her mouth before she could go on.

"Brett," he replied, looking over at her. "What's troubling you?"

"I need to send some money to Ma," she said. "Could you advance me twenty dollars on my pay so I can get it to her right away?"

His brow creased as he looked at her anxious face. "They're in dire need, aren't they." It was more of a statement than a question.

She nodded, her lips pressed together.

He pulled his tally book from his shirt pocket. "I'm going into Rosita tomorrow," he said, slipping off the rubber band. "There's a Western Union there. Give me her name, and I'll wire the money to her. She'll have it within a few hours."

Katie blinked. She'd dreaded asking, but now she wondered why she had. "Her name is Betsy Priestly," she said. Immediately, her breath stopped. Gasping, she rushed on. "She's actually my husband's mother. She's at the Tumbling P Ranch west of Muddy Creek."

"What's your husband's name?" Brett asked, sliding the tally book back into his pocket. "I may know him."

CHAPTER 3

"Johnny," Katie replied. How could the lies fall off her tongue so easily? She hated herself for it, but she was on a dangerous sled ride and couldn't get off.

Brett continued his bookwork and didn't say anything more. Finishing her duties, Katie stoked the fire in the stove and went to her room. She was too ashamed to talk to Brett anymore tonight. He was a good man, and she had never felt so lowdown in her entire life.

A woman of strong faith, Betsy Priestly had tried to instill that trust into her children. When Katie was nine years old, she had accepted Christ at her mother's knee. For the next eight years, her mother's prayers had been something she took for granted, like the sunrise or the cold spring behind their house.

That was before their lives had changed in a few short days last summer. When their cows began dropping in the fields by the dozens, Ma had prayed. Pa and the children prayed, too. They'd prayed and prayed while they watched their livelihood disintegrate in the cleansing fires that burned the swollen carcasses and their barn and everything else the cows had come near.

They'd prayed, and the garden had produced twice as much this year as any year before. Pa and Johnny had shot meat, and they'd had plenty.

But then harvest time was over. Wild game moved into winter hiding. Again, they'd prayed, but this time the heavens were silent.

"Don't lose hope," Ma had said twenty times a day. "God will see us through."

Katie had tried to hold onto her faith. Truly she had. Then Pa went away, but no money came. For weeks and weeks they'd prayed, but it never did come. *Where was God then?* she wondered in the most secret place in her heart. *Where is He now?*

Closing her bedroom door, she quickly changed into her flannel gown and lay down on her bed. The room was warmer tonight, the quilt soft and the pillow welcoming. She closed her eyes. *I'm going to sleep,* she told herself. She almost believed it until the wetness of her pillow made it cling to her cheek. *Oh, Lord,* she cried in her spirit, *where are*

You now?

Katie was up early the next morning and had the fire going before Brett appeared through the sitting-room door. "Morning," he said. "Duffy and I will be leaving before the men come for breakfast. Could you feed us something that's quick to make and pack a couple of sandwiches to take along?"

"Of course," she said.

He reached for his buffalo coat. "I'll saddle my horse while you're doing that." He opened the door and strode out, still settling his hat onto his head.

Duffy appeared shortly afterwards. "It's going to turn cold tonight," he predicted. "I can feel it in my bones." Without another word, he followed Brett.

Katie involuntarily shivered as the second cold blast hit her through that open door. Hurrying to her bedroom, she found her coat and ran out to the henhouse.

When Brett and Duffy arrived, she had six eggs scrambled and waiting for them with two day-old biscuits and some fresh, crisp bacon. She set their plates before them and poured steaming coffee into their mugs.

Duffy set his round hat on the table beside his plate. "Say, I could get used to this," he said. He paused while Brett said the blessing then sipped coffee. "That goes down just right, don't it?"

Brett methodically emptied his plate and his cup without talking, but that didn't stop Duffy's chatter. "There's snow in the air," he said. "Mark my words. I kin smell it."

The men finished about the same time and stood to leave. Katie handed Brett a tin of biscuit-and-bacon sandwiches. He thanked her and said, "We'll be back before suppertime, Lord willing."

"Thank you kindly for that breakfast, Katie," Duffy said with a loose-lipped smile. "If you wasn't already married, I'd have my proposal all writ out and memorized." He chuckled at his own joke and followed Brett out the door.

Katie stood beside the kitchen counter a moment to watch them go. Ma should have her money by tomorrow. With her first paycheck, she'd buy some writing paper and write Ma and the kids a letter.

Before she knew it, Katie had been there two full weeks. Now that the kitchen was clean and in good order, she enjoyed her work. The hours were long, but the company was good. She looked forward to meal times for the fun of listening to the hands' teasing and bantering with each other. She also looked forward to Brett's evening visits to the kitchen. Some days he worked over his account books and others he simply read his Bible.

One evening near the middle of November, she was giving the stove a final wipe-down for the night when she worked up the nerve to ask him to read aloud.

"What would you like me to read?" he asked. "Do you have a favorite passage?"

She paused with her cloth in mid-swipe. "Oh, I have lots of favorites. Psalm 23, Psalm 51, Psalm 127, lots of them."

"Are you a Christian?" he asked, watching her keenly.

Suddenly shy, she nodded. "I received Christ when I was nine years old. But there's no church near our place, so we never could go to church much."

He thumbed through the worn pages. "We don't have one near here either, unfortunately. A circuit rider comes through once a year or so." He stopped at a page. "Here's one. 'I will lift up mine eyes unto the hills, from whence cometh my help. My help cometh from the LORD, which made heaven and earth. He will not suffer thy foot to be moved: he that keepeth thee will not slumber.' " He read on to the end of Psalm 121.

She listened to his smooth voice and those

words sank into her soul.

When he finished, he said, "Katie, I've been thinking of something." He pulled his lips inward then dragged his lower lip out from between his teeth. "If you'd rather not, just say so. You don't have to do it."

"What is it?" she asked.

"Would you mind adding to your duties for an extra ten dollars a month? I'd be obliged if you'd clean my quarters once a week. That is, if you don't mind."

An extra ten dollars when she'd already bargained him up to forty? Fifty dollars a month seemed like a king's ransom. "I'd be glad to," she said. "I'll do it on Saturday mornings."

"Good," he replied, that small smile on his face. He nodded. "Good. Thank you." He turned a page in the Bible and began to read again.

At noon the following day, Katie was on the stoop ready to signal for dinner when Duffy rode into the yard on his blue roan mare. Katie waved at him, then stared. As he drew near, the tinkling of a tiny bell reached her. It grew louder until she realized the sound was coming from Duffy's saddle. He had a small bell tied under the pommel. As long as she'd been around cowboys, she'd never known anyone to put a bell on his saddle before.

Remembering her manners, she stopped staring and jangled the triangle. As always, her five boys came on the double. Grinning at their hurry, she stepped inside to get out of their way while they washed up at the pump.

When they were all seated and Brett had offered thanks, Katie handed a bowl of fried potatoes to Lew and looked at Duffy. "Duffy, why do you have a bell on your saddle? I've never seen that before."

Rollie gave a loud hoot. "I can answer that one," he said, handing her the platter of fried chicken. "We put a bell on him because one of these days he's going to forget how to come home and we'll need to be able to go out and find him."

That brought up a general howl. Duffy laughed with the rest. When the commotion died down, the old-timer said, "He's teasing you, Katie. Don't pay him no mind."

She glanced at Rollie's freckled face and said, "I stopped doing that the first day I came."

That brought another uproar.

Rollie grinned at her. "Nice shot, Katie, my gal. I didn't know you had it in you."

She smiled and picked up her fork. "Save some room, boys," she said. "I baked bread pudding. It's still warm, and there's cream to put over it."

Lew said, "You're spoiling us."

"Don't talk her out of it," Rollie told him. "She's doing just fine."

Katie glanced down the table and found Brett smiling at her. Not one of his usual small smiles, but a wide, big, natural smile. He met her gaze, and her heart stepped up its pace. That smile reached his eyes, too.

Suddenly, she realized what she was doing. A married woman shouldn't be so pleased at the way a man looked at her. It wasn't fitting.

She got up to serve dessert, a wonderful excuse to leave the table for a few minutes and calm her treacherous heart. She didn't look at him again, not once until the men all went outside.

That's the end of that, she told herself as she washed up after the meal. No more smiling and definitely no more looking.

That evening Brett came to the kitchen with his Bible in hand. He sat down and read for a few minutes, then said, "I'm going into Rosita tomorrow with Rollie and Hank, so I'm going to pay your first month's wages tonight." He pulled some coins from his shirt pocket. "Here's the thirty I still owe you. Is there anything you need from town?"

"You can send another twenty to Ma," she said. "There are a few things I need. Can I make a little list?" She opened a cabinet door. "There are a few things we need for the kitchen, too."

"Whatever you say," he replied absently, turning pages. "Put whatever you need on a list, and I'll bring it home." He stopped and ran his finger down a column. "How about Isaiah 40 for tonight?"

Her work was finished, so she sat at the table a few chairs away from him while he read. He spoke the words like he meant them: " 'Even the youths shall faint and be weary, and the young men shall utterly fall: But they that wait upon the LORD . . .' "

When he finished, he quietly said, "How about if we pray?"

She nodded, and he said, "Lord, You know how weak and needy we are. We're working hard and doing our best to scratch out a living out here in the wilderness. Please look down on us and bless us. Help us to stay close to You. Help us to speak a word for You when You give us a chance. Please help the Priestly family. They've had a bad time, Lord. Meet their needs, I pray. In the name of Jesus, amen."

Katie kept her head bowed after he said, "Amen." She felt tears building behind her eyelids, and she didn't want him to see. Finally, she pulled her handkerchief from her pocket and pressed it against her eyes.

When she looked up, the Bible was closed, and Brett sat quietly with his hands in his lap. His eyes were open, but his head was bowed.

She sniffed and scraped her chair back. "Thank you, Brett," she faltered. "Good night." She turned and escaped to her room. Lying on top of the quilt fully dressed, she curled into a tight ball and sobbed. She could see them so plainly — Bonnie and Mark, almost teenagers with their dark wounded eyes and a set to their young jaws that told of their determination to survive, Georgina, with her crooked braids and boundless energy, and Arlene, so gentle and sweet. She missed them all so.

Rubbing the heels of her hands into her burning eyelids, she reached down to pull her coat over her, snuggled into her pillow, and fell into a deep and troubled sleep. She dreamt of wild animals chasing Georgina, of Arlene lost in the dark, of Ma crying at night. When she awoke she felt like she'd hardly closed her eyes.

The men were riding out early that morning, so she had to get moving. Her bones ached, and so did her feet. She'd worn her shoes all night.

What can I give the men to take along for a nooning on the trail? she wondered as she quickly combed her hair. There was a large piece of bread pudding left. That would do for starters.

Moving automatically, she went out to add small sticks to the orange coals in the cook stove. While she waited, she found the tin for packing food and went to the counter to put the bread pudding inside it.

Suddenly, she blinked and wondered if she were still dreaming. The pan of bread pudding was completely empty, like someone had licked it clean. Had one of the men come in for a midnight snack? Maybe.

She stopped to add bigger wood to the fire and put on the coffeepot. Beef sandwiches would have to do for them today. Not that they minded much. She went to the box on the back porch where they set food to keep it cold and lifted the lid. It was empty. Even the plate was gone.

A knot formed inside her chest. Something was very wrong.

Katie headed for the sitting-room door and knocked. Brett appeared thirty seconds later, his face half covered with white lather, his straight razor in his hand.

"Someone took food from the back porch," she said. "I had a big piece of roast beef out there. I was going to make you beef sandwiches for the trail. When I went out, the box was empty."

"It could have been a raccoon," he said. "This time of year, they turn into real scoundrels."

"Would a raccoon take the plate, too?" she asked.

"Now, you've got a point there," he said. He waved the straight razor in the air near his right ear. "Would you mind if I finish shaving? I'll come back as soon as I'm through."

A giggle burst out. "I'm sorry. I guess I got pretty spooked."

He grinned. "Who wouldn't?"

Half an hour later, the three men bound for Rosita had gathered in the kitchen. They were drinking coffee and eating cornmeal mush.

Katie picked up the bread-pudding pan. "Did anyone finish this off?" she asked. "A large piece was in this corner last night, and now it's clean."

Rollie and Hank shook their heads.

Brett looked thoughtful. "Check with Duffy and Lew," he said. "If neither one of

47

them took it, have Duffy put a couple of hooks on the kitchen doors. I don't like the idea of someone coming inside."

"It could be an Indian," Hank said, spreading butter on a slab of bread.

"Or a drifter," Rollie added.

Letting out a harsh sigh, Brett looked disgusted. "What's the world coming to? Worried about strangers coming in at night. A body should be safe inside his own four walls."

Katie's eyes widened. "How about my door?" she asked Brett. "Could I have a lock on my door, too?"

He looked at her surprised. "Of course you can. Just mention it to Duffy. He'd crawl through an ice floe without his shirt on if you asked him to."

Sniggers went up from the younger men.

Brett ignored them. "When Lew and Duffy come to breakfast, ask them about the bread pudding. It's possible one of them raided the kitchen in the middle of the night."

But when she asked them an hour later, both men shook their heads.

"It must have been a drifter," Duffy said, rubbing the fuzz on the top of his head.

"But this area is so sparsely populated," Lew objected. "They usually like to stay closer to towns." He pulled out a chair and sat at the table.

Duffy's white eyebrows came low over his frosty blue eyes. "Whoever it was, he's had his last night of fun on us," he declared. "I'll get those hooks attached right after breakfast."

CHAPTER 4

Katie was on edge for the rest of the day. Walking to the henhouse, she had the skin-crawling sensation that someone was watching her. An hour later, she dropped a cupful of milk on the floor while she was making cornbread.

At noon, Duffy dipped a wedge of cornbread into his stew and said, "I scouted around the yard and found nary a sign of footprints. The ground is froze hard, but there should still be some sign." He shook his head. "Nothing."

Lew hooked his long arm around the back of his chair. "It was probably someone passing through and needing grub for his journey. Most likely, he won't be back."

Duffy nodded. "Those hooks should take the wind outta his sails, anyway."

Brett and his men returned shortly before supper. Rollie had a young buck thrown over the front of his saddle. He veered off from the rest of the men and circled the house to carry the meat to the smokehouse in back.

Venison would be a nice change from beef. Katie knew a recipe for barbeque using molasses and vinegar. It was Johnny's favorite, her pa's, too.

Brett came directly to the house and ground-hitched his horse near the kitchen steps. Katie saw him dismount. She hurried to turn her potatoes sizzling in a skillet before he walked in.

He carried a canvas sack and a package wrapped in brown paper and tied with twine. He set the goods on the table. "Here's your receipt for the money transfer," he said, digging into his shirt pocket for the paper. He handed it to her. "How have things been around here?"

Thanking him, she took the page and glanced at it. "Duffy put on the hooks. He said there are no tracks around the house at all. He can't understand how someone could have been prowling around without leaving any sign."

Brett's tired features creased with concern. "I'll have a talk with him." He hesitated. "I'm sorry about this. If you're feeling nervous, don't be afraid to ask for help, even if it's just going to get the eggs."

"I'm all right," she said. "Lew thinks it was a traveler, passing through and needing food for the trail."

"He's probably right." He backed away. "I'd best tend to my horse." He turned and headed outside, his boots loud on the plank floor.

Katie pushed the receipt into her skirt pocket and picked up the metal spatula. Maybe she was making too much of nothing.

Rollie was the first one in for supper. He turned a chair backwards, straddled it, and sat down. "What's the news on our food thief?" he asked.

Lifting a cloth-lined bowl full of hot biscuits to set them on the table, Katie said, "No news at all, I'm afraid." She told him of Duffy's unsuccessful search.

Rollie reached into the pocket of his blue flannel shirt. "I brought you something from town," he said. He handed two small paper envelopes toward her.

She hesitated then took them. "What are they?" she asked. If these were something personal, she'd have to refuse.

"Cinnamon and nutmeg," he said. "They'd just got some in, and I've got a powerful hankering for sweet rolls or maybe some pumpkin pies."

She sniffed the bits of brown paper. The aroma brought up several delightful images. "That's thoughtful of you, Rollie," she said. Carrying them to a cabinet, she opened a tin and carefully set the papers inside. "I'll see what I can do with those."

When Duffy came in, Rollie stood to turn his chair around and set it back to the table. "Say, Katie," he said, grinning. "I know why Duffy has a bell on his saddle."

The old-timer took off his hat. "I can't wait to hear this one," he said as Lew and Hank stepped through the door.

Rollie went on. "Hank put the bell on there so's old Duffy can't sneak up on us. We can say anything we want about him and be sure he's too far away to hear."

Lew chuckled. Hank tapped the back of Rollie's head with his palm, and Rollie grabbed Hank's wrist.

Duffy shook his head. "That was good, Rollie," he said. "Go to the head of the class."

Hank chuckled. "Yeah, that's where the dunce sits on a stool."

Brett arrived, and Katie took her place at a far corner of the table. The banter died down while Brett prayed, then began again soon after his amen.

"How about a game of checkers after supper?" Duffy asked Lew.

The big man shook his head. "I'm turning in early."

The old-timer scanned the table for another likely opponent.

"I'll play," Brett told him, "after I finish my accounts."

While the men played their game, Hank entertained them all with his fiddle. He didn't play that well, but any music was a welcome diversion. Watching the checker game, Rollie sang a few bars now and then.

Katie took her time finishing the dishes. She wiped every surface and fed her sourdough starter. Setting out a large pan of apple-pandoughty for the men to snack on, she said good night and went to her room. The excitement of that day had worn her out. She wanted some time alone before she retired.

In her packages, she'd found a writing tablet and two sharpened pencils along with her change. She wanted to start a letter home tonight. She'd write a little every day until one of the men want back to town to mail it for her.

She left the door open, so the warmth of the kitchen stove could come in. Lighting the lamp, she folded back the cardboard cover on the tablet and wrote the date in careful script: November 18, 1884. She began by telling all about the ranch and the hands. She told how much she liked working there and about Johnny's job in Musgrove.

Her eyes were drooping by the time she finished the back of the second page. She closed the tablet, slid it under her thin mattress, and shut her door. Thank the Lord for Duffy and this new hook. She'd sleep better with it there. A few minutes later, she snuggled in her warm flannel gown under the quilt and closed her eyes. Sleep covered her like a goose-down comforter.

Suddenly, she came full awake. The room was black as ink. The house was silent except for the normal creaks.

Katie lay motionless, her eyes wide, her ears tuned for the slightest sound. All she heard was the rattling of the wind against her windowpane.

Turning over, she pulled the quilt closer around her neck. If someone was out there, she was the last person to check. Let the men see to it.

After a few minutes, she dozed and didn't wake up until morning.

She was dressed and in the kitchen a few minutes past five, moving mechanically to build up the fire and put on coffee. Crossing to the table to gather the mugs and plates left from the men's late snack, she suddenly stiffened. The apple-pandoughty was completely gone, the dish licked clean.

She let the pan stay where it was.

When Brett came in a few minutes later, she pointed at the table. "Did the men finish that whole pan last night?" she asked, a hint of accusation in her voice.

Brett looked from the object in question to her pointing finger. "Well, yes. I believe they did." He looked a little sheepish. "I'm afraid I ate four pieces myself."

Blinking, she let out a great sigh of relief. "I was afraid someone had been in here last night."

He went on. "I made a fresh pot of coffee after you turned in. Me and the boys had a time eating pandoughty and swapping stories until late. It must have been nine o'clock when we called it a day."

She held up her hand with the palm toward him. "That's all right. I don't mind if you ate it. That's not it at all."

He grinned. "Maybe I should leave a note from now on: Here lies an empty pan left by five hungry cowpokes."

She chuckled at his foolishness. "I've got to get busy or breakfast will be late." She picked up the lard can. "Would you mind bringing in that last haunch of beef from the smokehouse? It'll have to thaw awhile before I can cut it up."

"Sure thing," he said, picking up his coat.

She handed him a basin, then opened the cupboard door to find the flour bin.

Brett had his hand on the door latch when she said, "Brett, didn't you buy a fresh sack of cornmeal yesterday?"

"That's right."

"I'm sure I put it right here," she said, her hand on the empty shelf. She turned to look at him. "It's gone."

"What?" he demanded. In two strides, he was next to her, peering into the cabinet.

She opened all the doors. No cornmeal anywhere.

He said, "You'd best check through all the cabinets and see if anything else is missing. I'm getting mighty tired of this, and that's a fact."

Picking up the basin, he headed outside. He was back in five minutes, the enamel basin hanging from his hand. "The beef's gone," he said. He set the bowl on the table.

Still stirring biscuit dough, Katie felt her throat tighten. There *had* been someone inside last night, latched doors or no.

The breakfast mood was somber that morning. The men poured sausage gravy over their biscuits and forked them down while Brett talked. "The doors were still locked when I came in the kitchen this morning," he said. "I can't figure it out, but we've got to put a stop to it."

Duffy said, "Should we set up a guard?"

Brett replied, "I hate to think of watching through the night. That would be hard on all of us."

"Maybe it's a ghost," Hank said, only half joking. "How could a person come through a latched door?"

Brett's lips twisted. "Does a ghost need to eat?" he asked. "Could a ghost take food through the door with him?" He turned to Katie. "Just exactly what was taken last night? Did you figure that out?"

She nodded and listed off, "Five pounds of cornmeal, a small jug of sour milk, and a cooking pot."

Rollie said, "Someone's hiding out. They're getting hungry, and we're the grocery store."

Katie swallowed. "An escaped prisoner, do you think?"

Brett said, "It's not likely, but it is possible. The closest jail is in Pueblo. A man on foot could cover the distance in a couple of weeks, I reckon."

"This time of year?" Duffy asked. "I'd

think a man in that shape would head south and get out of the state the quickest way he could. He'd hop a train, most likely."

Duffy shook his head. "It's going to turn bitter cold. Whoever it is out there can't make it much longer."

Rollie said, "If you can spare me, I'll scout around on horseback today, looking for tracks."

"Take the whole morning, if you need it," Brett said. "We're going to be working the fence line south by the spring. You can ride out to meet us when you're finished." He scraped back his chair. Before he stood, he said, "On second thought, Rollie, just come back to the house when you're through, in case Katie needs something. I don't like to have her here alone with all this going on."

Rollie nodded, and Katie breathed for the first time that morning.

She tried to go about her usual chores as though nothing had happened, but her attention was elsewhere. She burned the first batch of sourdough bread, not badly, but enough to make her irritated at herself.

When Rollie came in, she was scrubbing the kitchen floor. At least that was something that couldn't be botched.

"Mind your feet," she said as he stepped inside. "Take big steps and sit down at the table. I'll bring you a hot cup of coffee in a few minutes."

He took off his coat and hat then did as she said. Sitting down, he propped his boots on the chair across from him and said, "My mama would chase us out of the house with the mop handle if we stepped on her wet floor. She's a terror, my mother is." He grinned. "She raised six of us boys and not a scoundrel among us."

Katie sat back on her heels and smiled at him. "She sounds like my kind of woman. I have been known to chase the young'uns outside from time to time."

He said, "Do you have children?"

"My brothers and sisters," she said, leaning down to wipe the cloth over the floorboards. "There are six of us, four girls and two boys. I have an older brother and the rest are younger."

"You married young," he said. "You can't be more than sixteen yourself."

"Eighteen," she corrected. She clamped her mouth shut. She was talking way too much.

Finishing the mopping, she carried the bucket to the back step and flung the dirty water to the ground. She set the bucket on the porch beside the door and returned to Rollie in the kitchen.

"Did you find anything?" she asked as she poured his coffee.

He shook his head. "Duffy was right. Whoever it is, he knows enough to cover his tracks." She set the mug in front of him, and he picked it up. "That could be Indians."

She gulped. "You think so?"

Glancing at her face, he said, "I'm guessing. I don't know anything for sure." He took his time looking around the kitchen. "Is there any place else that a man could come through?"

"I've been thinking about that myself," she said, her arms crossed tightly about her waist. "This room is tight. I checked it out myself."

He drained his cup and set it down. "I'm going to look around the smokehouse. Maybe the fellow made a mistake out there and left a shoeprint or a hoofprint." He paused beside the door. "Don't worry, Katie. We're going to watch out for you. Believe me, not a man here wants anything to happen to you. You saved our lives, you know that? You surely did. If you weren't already married, I'd lay odds that you'd have three or four proposals by now." With that he went out and closed the door firmly behind him.

Katie rubbed her forehead. Well, that proved Brett had known what he was doing when he made that rule about no single women. Not that she wasn't flattered, but on this side of things she was very glad she didn't have to fend anyone off. She could be just friends with all of them.

That evening at supper, Brett announced that there would be no guard unless it was absolutely necessary. "Keep in mind that you may have to miss some sleep before this is all over," he told them. "I'd suggest you all turn in early."

However, the night was calm. Nothing awakened Katie. She felt rested and refreshed when she arrived in the kitchen the next morning. The weather had suddenly grown a little milder, so her feet weren't quite as cold. Maybe she'd stir up some hotcakes this morning. The boys would like that.

Stoking the fire, she put out her hand to pick up the coffeepot and fill it. A cold wave traveled down her back, sucking her breath from her. The blue enamel coffeepot was gone.

CHAPTER 5

Brett came immediately in response to her banging on the sitting-room door. He had a towel draped around his neck. One look at her and he said, "What is it? Are you all right?"

When she didn't answer right away, he covered her hands with his. His fingers were warm.

"The coffeepot!" she croaked. Her throat was too tight to say more.

He rushed past her to the cook stove and looked at its bare top. Suddenly, he snapped the towel from around his neck and flung it to the floor. "Duffy!" he bellowed.

He strode to the bunkhouse door and tore it open. "Duffy!" He charged inside, leaving the door ajar behind him.

Katie moved aside to be out of the line of sight. The last thing she wanted was for one of the hands to see her peering into their quarters as they rolled out of bed.

She stood near the stove, her hands twisted inside her apron. What was she going to do now? A missing cooking pan and now the coffeepot — at this rate, she was going to have to get creative or stop cooking altogether. If she had any food left to cook, that is.

Men's sleepy voices drifted out of their quarters until someone had the sense to close the door to the bunkhouse.

Katie found a saucepan. She poured coffee grounds into it, then filled it with water and added a few eggshells. It would probably taste like mud, but at least they'd have coffee for breakfast.

The men drifted into the kitchen long before she was ready to signal that the meal was ready. Lew carried a dented tin coffeepot. He handed it to her. "This is from our trail pack," he said. "It's not very big, but you can use it until we can get to town and buy another one."

She took the scuffed and stained pot. "Thank you," she said and set it on the washing-up counter. It looked as though it had been rubbed with sand the last time it had been used.

Despite the impropriety, Katie considered asking Brett if she could sleep in one of his rooms until all this was over. She felt so alone and out of reach in her own place. If someone tried to storm her door down, would anyone hear her call for help?

Brett came in and told her, "This morning we'll do the chores *after* we eat. First, the men and I have to powwow."

When everyone was at the table, Brett poured coffee from the saucepan into five mugs. "Let it set awhile to settle the grounds," he told the men as he handed the cups around, then he joined them at the table.

Still frying bacon, Katie listened to their talk.

Duffy said, "I believe we can rule out a few things, boss. Indians don't give two wooden nickels about coffee nor coffeepots."

Lew added, "Drifters almost always carry a camp coffeepot. They wouldn't have no use for a big kitchen pot like ours. Besides, they don't stay in one place too long. It's nigh onto zero degrees out there. They wouldn't be camping out around here. They'd want to find a place closer to civilization where there are other men to share a fire with and more places to scrounge for food."

Brett nodded. "So, no Indians and no drifters. What does that leave us?"

"Someone on the run," Hank said. "An outlaw or a convict."

Duffy shook his head. "Someone on the run would keep on running. This has been going on for more than a week."

An idea suddenly came to Katie. She turned from the stove to speak. "Someone in trouble," she said, feeling her stomach contract in sympathetic hunger pains. "Someone destitute."

The men sat in silence for a few minutes.

Brett lifted his coffee cup and tried out a sip. He grimaced and set it down. "If there's someone in genuine trouble, we have to find out who it is, so we can give some proper help. He'll freeze to death out there if we get a blizzard or a real bad cold spell. Last winter it got down to thirty below."

He turned to Lew. "You and Duffy take off for town after the meal," he told him. Turning toward Katie, he went on, "Make them a list of supplies to buy for the kitchen and give it to them. Get plenty."

Back to the men, he said, "Rollie, scout around the outside of the ranch grounds. Look for hiding places where there's shelter from the cold. He'd need a fire, and he'd need water nearby. Think it through from that angle and see what you can come up with."

Katie set bacon and eggs on the table along with a plate of sliced bread. Brett bowed and prayed, "Lord, if there is someone hungry hiding outside in the cold, please help us to find him. We've got room in the bunkhouse, and we've got plenty to eat. But for Your protecting hand, we'd have lost our cattle and everything here. Thank You for Your care. Amen."

Katie picked up her fork and tasted the eggs. They were cooked to perfection, but she couldn't force herself to swallow more than one bite. Mercifully, the meal was over soon and the hands dispersed to begin their day.

Katie got out of her seat to clear the table. Still in his chair, Brett slowly sipped his coffee. When she came near him to pick up Hank's dishes, he said, "Sit down for a minute, will you? Please?"

She glanced at him, surprised, and sank into Hank's chair at the corner beside him.

"I'm getting a little worried about you," he said gently. "Are you afraid of staying in here alone?"

Avoiding his gaze, she nodded. "A couple of times I woke up thinking I heard someone come in, but I've been too scared to cry out. He could come and get me next."

He nodded. "I know. I thought about that

myself." His mouth worked outward as he considered that. "We'll have to come up with some kind of signal so you can alert me without giving yourself away at the same time. I'll talk it over with Duffy when he comes back from town."

Watching her hands knotted together in her lap, she nodded. "Thank you."

He made a move to push his chair back.

She looked up. "Brett . . ."

He stopped, waiting for her to go on.

"Would you mind if I . . ." she paused, nervous about asking him.

"Probably not," he murmured with that small smile. "Go on."

"Could I start setting some stuff out for him? Cooked leftovers and things like that?" She met his gaze for the first time. "It makes me feel sick inside, thinking about someone starving out in the cold."

He cocked his head so one eye focused on her and the other eye squinted. "You know what they say about feeding strays," he drawled.

"This is a human being, not a dog," she retorted. She clamped her lips shut. That statement was far too forceful.

He smiled, his blue-green eyes scanning her face for a long moment. "You're thinking about your own family, aren't you?"

She nodded.

He placed both his hands flat on the table. "Go ahead. Between all of us, we should be able to smoke him out, so we can bring him in out of the cold altogether." He stood and picked up his coat. "Hank and I are going to ride the fence line today to check for breaks. We may not be back in time for dinner."

Standing, too, she nodded. "I'll save the main meal until this evening."

He put on his coat and hat then stood near the door, unmoving, watching her.

Wondering why he'd hesitated, she looked up at him. Those blue-green eyes held hers for an endless moment, so full of concern, so warm and . . .

Suddenly, she gasped. "I have a letter! I almost forgot it. Tell Duffy to come and pick it up before he goes." She scurried toward her room, then remembered her manners and called back, "Please!"

He chuckled. The door banged as he went out.

Her hands were shaking as she pulled out the paper tablet. Her knees were weak as she tore out the pages with writing on them. What was wrong with her? She'd told herself, no more looking, and what had she done? Gone right ahead and looked anyway.

She let her head fall back until her chin pointed at the ceiling. Closing her eyes, she drew in a deep breath. *He thinks you are a married woman! Start acting like it!*

Folding the five pages together, she realized she didn't have an envelope. She dug in her coat pocket for the coins Brett had given her weeks ago.

She sat on the edge of her bed for a few more minutes, forcing calmness through her clenched hands and tense mouth. Nothing had happened between her and the boss. It was all in her foolish, stupid mind.

When Duffy arrived fifteen minutes later, she had everything neatly on the counter waiting for him. She handed him the pages and pointed to the top sheet. "I've written everything here," she told him. "If you would buy two envelopes, you can address one to my mother and bring the other one back to me for next time." She gave him a coin. "Here's five dollars. It's the smallest amount I've got."

He slid the letter into his inside coat pocket. "Is there anything else you need from town?" he asked. "Besides a coffeepot, that is?"

She nodded. "Cornmeal, lard, and pinto beans." She paused then went on. "Use some of my money to buy a wool army blanket."

"I kin remember that," he said, nodding. "We'd best get there and back in a hurry. We're in for some snow any time now. I don't hanker on getting caught in a blizzard."

She handed him a cloth bundle. "Here's something to eat while you're on the trail. It's not much, but I wasn't expecting you to be riding out again so soon."

He took it from her. "I'm obliged, Katie," he said. "You're number one in my book."

She smiled. If he had been her natural-born uncle, she would have hugged him. "You're very welcome, Duffy," she said.

Grinning, he repositioned his floppy hat and shuffled out.

Deep in thought, Katie cleared away the remains of breakfast. Brett was so patient even through all this trouble. What lay under that silent, gentle exterior? Suddenly, she had an overwhelming urge to find out.

The day passed in peace and silence. Katie stayed busy baking bread and cleaning Brett's part of the house. She liked to clean when he was away. Handling his things with him looking on was too embarrassing. When she finished, the floors glowed with a fresh coating of linseed oil and the fireplace stones had a brilliant sheen.

She saw Rollie ride in shortly after three o'clock that afternoon. Ten gleaming golden loaves made a double line down the back counter, filling the house with a rich aroma.

He went into the barn for a few minutes, then sauntered to the house. Despite his short stature, he walked like a big man with his chest out and his head high. He came inside and unbuttoned his denim coat. "Boy, if that don't smell good!" he said, eyeing the loaves set out to cool.

Katie asked, "Did you find anything?"

"Nothing I could say for sure," he said, taking off his black flat-crowned hat. "Whoever it is, he knows something about tracking. Otherwise, he'd leave more traces of his coming and going. The average person would." He looked at the stove. "Have you got any coffee?"

"I've got better than that," she replied. She pulled a dish towel off a large pan of warm sweet rolls and set the pan on the table.

With a gasp of anticipation, he pulled out the head chair and sat down. Katie brought him a plate and a steaming mug of coffee. She left him alone for a full ten minutes while she finished peeling potatoes for supper.

Finally, she joined him and helped herself

to a sweet roll. It was buttery and warm. "This is some of that cinnamon you brought me," she said. Reaching for a second one, she giggled. "We're spoiling our supper."

He laughed. "I won't tell if you won't." He drained his coffee cup and stood to refill it from the camp pot on the stove.

"Rollie," Katie began when he sat down, "where is Brett from? Originally, I mean. Is he from Colorado?"

"Wyoming," he said, draining the second cup of coffee. "Far as I know, his parents still live there."

"I wonder what brought him down here."

"Why don't you ask him?" he said, standing. "It's late. I'd best see to the stock. Thanks for the rolls!" With that he lifted his hat and coat and strode out.

An hour later, Duffy and Lew rode in. Duffy came directly to the kitchen without even taking his horse to the barn. He set a burlap sack on the table. "Here's the goods you needed," he said. Reaching into his inner pocket, he pulled out two envelopes. "These are for you."

Katie took them. The first was the new envelope she'd asked for. The second was thick with her name scrawled on the outside of it — a letter from home.

Hurrying to her room, she tore it open

and sat on her bed to read it. It was in her mother's handwriting.

Dear Katie,

I'm so glad to have good news for you. I received a letter from your father last week along with forty dollars. He's been riding the rails in the caboose. His pay was delayed because of some kind of mix up, but he's all right. I got your twenty dollars as well, so the children and I are living like kings. We've plenty of food, and I bought some coal to keep us warmer. I hope you are well, my dear. Thank you so much for what you are doing for us. I haven't heard from Johnny yet. I hope he's doing all right. Please write me when you can.

All my love,
Ma

Katie held the page to her heart and breathed a heartfelt prayer of thanksgiving. The family would be fine. Next spring, they'd all come home and everything would get back to normal. Her shoes had wings when she returned to the kitchen. God really had heard their prayers. He really was there.

That night after supper, she waited for Brett to come into the kitchen, the same as she waited for him every night. That evening he brought in his account books to record the expenses from that day's trip to town.

Katie was used to his routine now. Those quiet moments after the supper dishes were finished had become her most cherished part of the day.

When he finished with his records, she joined him at the table. "Duffy brought me a letter," she said. "It was good news."

He leaned back in his chair and grinned. "You don't say. I'm glad to hear that."

"I just wanted to say thank you for giving me that advance. It made all the difference for Ma and the kids. She said they've got plenty to eat and she bought some coal, too."

"Well, I want to say thank you to you, too," he said. "You've turned this cold cow camp into a home, Katie. The food's good and the place is spotless. I couldn't ask for any better."

She beamed under his praise. "I like it here," she said. "The men are fun to be around."

"As you can probably tell, they like you, too."

"What made you choose Colorado?" she asked him. "Why did you buy land here?"

He tilted his head in that familiar way and

said, "I met a man in Cheyenne who wanted to sell. The price was right, and the land was good. So I bought it."

"Didn't you want to stay near your folks?"

He leaned back in his chair, his legs stretching straight out. "I'm the youngest of four boys. My three brothers are all married and have big families. I guess I figured they were enough family to take care of the folks." He quirked in the side of his mouth in a vaguely cynical smile. "Besides, every single girl in the territory had me on her list of possibles. I got tired of trying to outrun them."

She laughed at that.

He chuckled, too.

She said, "I would think you'd be flattered. Most young men would be thrilled."

He rubbed his five o'clock shadow. "I guess I'm too independent. I always figured I'd pick my own gal, not *get* picked." He shifted in his chair. "Say, I've been thinking that maybe we could set a little trap and catch our prowler."

She waited, listening.

"How about if you set a nice meal in that box on the back porch. The boys and I will take turns watching. When he comes, we'll grab him. It's that simple."

She looked sheepish. "I'm afraid I'm

ahead of you. After supper I put a new blanket on top of the box and a pan of sweet rolls inside it."

"You don't say!" He got to his feet. "Let's see if they're still there." He headed toward the back door with Katie behind him. He paused to lift the lantern from the center of the table as he passed it.

When he reached the porch, he stopped in the doorway and cried out. "I'll be a jackrabbit's hind leg!"

"What?" She edged past him.

The blanket was gone.

"If I was a betting man, I'd lay odds that the rolls are gone, too!"

Katie lifted the lid and gazed forlornly into the empty box. Disgusted, she dropped the lid. "I'm sorry. I should have told you what I was doing. We could have caught him and no one would have lost a wink of sleep."

Holding the lantern up so he could see her face, he said, "You're too quick to blame yourself. We'll try again tomorrow."

Standing so close to her that she could see the gold flecks in his eyes, he gave her that slow smile, and Katie forgot to breathe. For a moment she feared . . . no, hoped . . . he was going to kiss her.

Then he moved back, and the moment was gone.

Katie lifted her skirt to clear the doorsill and headed back inside.

Brett paused beside her bedroom door. "I hope Duffy's contraption works," he said, looking overhead at the string crossing the ceiling. It began next to Katie's bedstead and ended tied to a bell in Brett's bedroom. If she got scared, she could pull the string and, hopefully, it would ring and wake Brett up.

She stopped beside him to look at the string, too. She looked doubtful. "If I hear a noise, you'll find out if it works, all right. Unless you sleep right through it."

He grinned down at her. "I won't sleep through that. I promise you."

She suddenly became conscious of the man-smell from his blue flannel shirt, his collar open just below his Adam's apple, the warm look in his eyes.

Forcing herself to look away, she said, "Good night," and stepped into her room. She firmly closed the door and hooked the latch.

Leaning against the oak door, she rubbed her face with both hands. She could hear her mother's voice so clearly echoing in her head, "Oh, what a tangled web we weave . . ."

How was she going to get out of this?

Brett was the dearest, most desirable man she'd ever known. He was tall and strong and handsome. He was a Christian, true and honorable.

She closed her eyes and let out an anguished sigh. She was fighting a losing battle, and she'd better admit it now. She'd condemned herself by her own impulsive words. Brett thought she was married, and she was hopelessly in love with him.

CHAPTER 6

She dressed for bed and turned out the light. Under her thick covers, she closed her eyes. The best thing for her to do was to confess her lie to him before breakfast. That was the right thing to do. But did she have the courage to do it?

She knew she didn't. She was a hopeless coward without a speck of principle. When Brett found out the truth, he would probably turn her out. She deserved it, too.

Despite her agitation, she slept well and woke up early. She took her time dressing, thankful for a few extra minutes of quiet before the morning flurry of activity began.

Brett was already in the kitchen when she came in. The stove was glowing and the new coffeepot giving off steam.

"Good morning," she said, pausing at the end of the hallway. Just seeing him made her heart beat a little faster.

He looked up from reading his Bible.

"Good morning. Did you hear anything last night?"

She shook her head. "With those easy pickings he got last night, I'm not surprised. Why come back when you've already had a windfall?"

He nodded. "You're right about that."

She pulled out the flour sack and the tin of lard. "How about pancakes this morning?" she asked him.

"Duffy will be delighted," he said.

She looked at him and he smiled, a soft, gentle smile that was somehow different. Or maybe it was the tenderness in his eyes that was different.

Turning her back toward him, she used a metal cup to scoop flour from the bag.

"Maybe we'll get another deer today," he said. "Sometimes when we first go out, we'll spot one or two. Rollie can usually bring one down if he has a mind to."

"That would be good," she said. "The smokehouse is almost empty."

They chatted about the insignificant details that people usually talked about before breakfast, but Katie's mind was definitely not on their words. She couldn't wait for breakfast to be over so he'd ride out and she wouldn't have to watch her every syllable, fearing that she'd give herself away. Yet, at the same time, she wanted to throw her arms around him and beg him to stay with her forever.

She had serious fears that she was losing her mind.

Finally, the hands trooped in from the barn, chores finished and all of them famished. The usual *oohs* and *aahs* went up over the pancakes.

After the prayer, Rollie forked three tender, golden circles onto his plate. "Hey, I've got an announcement," he called out to no one in particular.

"Sandra Matins finally said yes," Hank called back.

Rollie smirked. "You think that's possible?" he demanded, a bit too hotly. He turned to Katie and said, "Sandra Matins is the daughter of Rosita's mayor. She doesn't condescend to notice a mere cowhand."

Hank called out, "He sure is sweet on her, though."

Rollie stuffed a triple-thick piece of sorghum-coated pancake into his mouth and chewed. Swallowing, he said, "What I meant to say was" — he gave a mock bow to Hank — "I know why Duffy has a bell on his saddle."

A chorus of groans went up.

Brett shook his head. "Hurry up and tell

us. You're killing us with suspense." He shifted in his chair and picked up his coffee cup.

Rollie laughed. "He uses it to turn his horse. When he taps it on the right side, the horse turns right, and when he taps it on the left side, the horse turns left." He waited, eyebrows raised.

The room was silent for several seconds. Finally Lew said, "Save your energy for the fence line, Barker. You'll do all of us more good."

Several chuckles followed.

Unruffled, Rollie reached for a second helping. "These are great, Katie," he said. "It's a shame you're married, 'cause —"

Brett interrupted him. "We know. We know," he called out, "but we're tired of hearing that one, too."

Rebuffed, Rollie clamped his mouth shut and poured sorghum.

Surprised at Brett's abrupt words, Katie stole a glance at him over the rim of her coffee cup. He had his face turned down, his attention fully on his food, so she couldn't get a good look at his expression.

She caught the cowhands exchanging looks over Brett's bowed head. Whatever that was about, they were as clueless as she was.

Half an hour later, the men rode out. Relieved, Katie watched them from the window. She had the whole day to herself. She needed some quiet to sort out her thoughts and calm down her treacherous emotions.

She picked up the broom to sweep through the entire kitchen and moved into Brett's quarters to sweep there, too. His bedroom was the back room closest to the kitchen, a room that was also large but spare. A wide bedstead took up the center of the space. Half of one wall held a row of pegs for hanging clothes and other items. The other side had a narrow dresser, and that was all. No rugs or curtains in this room either.

Using a dust rag to touch here and there as she made her way through, she finished his room and closed the door. Moving further, she opened the door that led to his office, not that he used it much. He almost always came to the kitchen with his books, saying that it was warmer in there.

Pushing inside, her eyes on the floorboards as the broom swished across them, she glanced up and froze. A scream formed at the back of her throat. She fought it down, her breath coming in small gasps at the effort.

The desk drawers had been pulled out to their maximum length, papers hanging out of them. The desktop had open books sprawled across it, some books pushed to the floor. Pens and pencils lay scattered across the floor as well.

Standing in the doorway for a long moment, Katie backed out and pulled the door closed behind her. She wouldn't touch anything until Brett had a chance to look at it. Besides, she wouldn't feel right touching his personal papers. How would she know where to put anything anyway?

Suddenly, she dropped the broom and dashed into the kitchen. Hooking the front and back doors, she made a circle around the room, testing every window and looking for weak spots where someone might be able to push in. She moved into Brett's quarters and did the same.

That's when she found it. The far window in his sitting room had a loose latch. It looked latched, but when she pulled on the lower sash, the latch slid away and the window moved up. That window faced the front porch, so it was easy enough to lift the window and step over the sill. The door to the kitchen had no latch. That single loose latch gave free access to the entire house.

Katie was as close to panic as she had ever

been in her entire life. She picked up the broom and returned to the kitchen. If the door had swung into the kitchen, she could have braced it shut by shifting the wood box over to block it. Unfortunately, it swung into the sitting room, so she'd have to hold the door closed somehow.

But how? She had no tools, no boards, and no nails.

There was no bell attached to Brett's horse for her to ring him home. It was still mid-morning. How could she get through the day?

The only safe place she knew of was her bedroom. At least it had a latch on the door.

She picked up the bag of potatoes and carried it into her room. The stew was already simmering. She only had to peel the potatoes. That wouldn't be too bad. She could mix up biscuits after they rode in.

She had planned to make some more pandoughty and scour the counters as well, but those things would have to wait.

Working with nervous haste, she peeled the potatoes. Dashing around the kitchen, she set them to wait in a pan of water and hurried back into her room. What could she do with herself within these four walls for half the day?

She ran into the kitchen for the broom

and other cleaning supplies and hurried back to latch herself in.

An hour later, the windows gleamed, the floors were clean enough for a baby to crawl on, and cobwebs had disappeared. *You're being an idiot,* she told herself as she stretched out on her bed. *No one has ever come into the house during the daytime.* Her eyes drifted closed. *What are you so worried about?*

The next thing she knew, the kitchen door banged, and Brett called out, "Katie?"

She flew off the bed, unlocked the door, and bolted into the kitchen. She met him in the center of the room and flung herself into his arms. Trembling, she clung to him.

"What on earth?" he said. "Did someone come in here while we were gone?"

She shook her head, her face buried in his buffalo coat.

Finally, she gasped. "I found out how he's getting in."

Gently loosening her grip on his waist, he said, "Show me. We'll take care of it right away." He kept his arm around her shoulders as she turned toward his quarters.

"I was sweeping up," she began, her voice faltering, "and I found your office . . ." She pointed toward the closed door.

He moved ahead of her to open it then

drew up, his eyebrows pulled down. "What was he looking for?" he demanded, moving inside the room.

Katie stayed in the doorway, her arms wrapped about her waist. She wasn't cold, but she was surely shivering. "That's not where he's getting in," she said.

Brett looked up from his examination of his desktop. "Where is it?" He moved toward her.

She walked to the offending window, opened it, and then closed it again.

He looked at the latch and worked the sash to see how it had loosened. "I'll have Duffy take care of that right away," he said. Opening the window, he bellowed, "Duffy! Come to the house!" then closed it again.

"I was too scared to stay in the kitchen," she said. She wanted to act calm, but she couldn't catch her breath. "I stayed in my room with the door locked."

"All day?" he asked. He seemed as upset about that as he had about his office. He put his arm around her shoulders, and she leaned against him. "Let's get you something hot to drink. I believe I have a tin of tea in the cabinet."

She nodded. "It's in the second door from the left."

"Well, you're going to sit at the table and

let me make you some," he said. "You're all in."

When they reached the kitchen door, Duffy burst in. "What's going on, boss?" he demanded, his eyes darting to Katie's face. "Did something happen?"

"No one was here," Brett told him, "but Katie's been scared half to death. She found a window with a loose latch. It's probably where the varmint has been getting inside. I want you to fix it right away." He jerked his head backward. "It's in there. The second window past the fireplace."

Duffy edged past them and disappeared through the door. Brett closed it after him, then stayed beside Katie until she sat at the table.

"I'm embarrassed," she managed to say. "I've heard stories of pioneer women fighting off bears or crawling through the brush for miles after they've been wounded. I feel like such a weakling."

He found the tin of tea and lifted it from the shelf. "Everyone's not cut from the same cloth," he said. He took off the lid and paused to smile at her. "There's no sense in blaming yourself because you're you, is there? God made you just the way He wanted you. I, for one, am glad He did."

He dipped up a cupful of hot water from

the pot on the stove and added tea leaves. Stirring it, he added a little molasses and brought it to her. "Here. This should make you feel better."

"Thank you." She let the warm steam cover her face for a moment before she sipped.

He sat near her. "I feel rotten for leaving you here without one of the men nearby. With all that's been going on around here lately, that was pure foolishness. I'm so sorry, Katie. Can you forgive me?" He said it so sincerely and so caringly that she had a strong urge to cry.

She didn't know what to say, so she simply nodded. Cupping her hands around the mug, she bent closer to its calming warmth.

In a few minutes, her trembling had stopped and her breathing slowed to normal. To say that she'd overreacted would be the understatement of the century. How would she ever live it down — throwing herself at Brett like that and clinging to him like a drowning man overboard in a hurricane?

He didn't seem to notice her fiery cheeks because he said, "We need to bait that trap again tonight. Do you think you're up to it?"

Relieved to have something to talk about,

she said, "Of course. I'll fix a plate with some of that stew and some biscuits. The smell alone should bring him down out of the hills."

Brett smiled. "Good." The front door to his quarters banged shut. "That's Duffy. I'll have him check all the other windows — in the bunkhouse and everywhere. I was so worried about the kitchen that I didn't check those other windows close enough. I just looked at them instead of trying every one." He shook his head. "I'm afraid I'm to blame for most of your distress, Katie. I can't tell you how sorry I am."

Uncomfortable, she got to her feet. "I'd best mix up those biscuits and get them into the oven," she said, turning away from him. She couldn't stop thinking about the feeling of his arms around her, the smell of his coat, the slow sound of his heartbeat against her ear. Yanking the mixing bowl from its shelf, she reached for the sack of flour. *You're pathetic,* she scolded herself. *Truly pathetic.*

An hour later, the men gathered for dinner. Katie set the pot of stew in the center of the table with a cloth-lined bowl of biscuits beside it, and they dug in.

Duffy started out the evening's conversation. "You don't have to worry about any more loose windows," he said, speaking to

Katie. "I double-checked every one of them, even in the bunkhouse."

Rollie said, "Good. Let's keep him out of the bunkhouse. We don't want no prowler catching Hank with his hair messed up."

Lew drawled, "Catching lead is more like it."

"I'd like to ask for a couple of volunteers," Brett said, reaching for a third biscuit. "We're going to lay a trap tonight, and someone's got to watch it. We'll take hour-long shifts. It's too cold out there to stay longer than that."

Lew nodded. "I've got first watch."

"Second," Hank said.

"I guess that makes me third," Rollie said. "I'd best get to bed right after supper."

Brett said, "We may not have to call on you, Rollie. Last time he had the box emptied before we turned in. I hope he's hungry tonight."

When the boys were finished, Katie filled a bowl with stew and placed two biscuits on top of it. She covered the whole thing with a dishtowel and handed it to Brett.

"When Lew's in place, I'll set it out," he told her, putting the bowl on the freshly wiped table. "No sense letting that varmint get the drop on us a second time."

Ten minutes later, Lew went out. Brett

followed a few minutes later.

Katie washed the dishes, alert for a shout or a scuffling noise from the back porch. She hung her towel to dry and pulled out the bag of beans.

Brett had just come to the kitchen with his Bible when a thud shook the house. Brett dashed for the back door.

Katie stayed in the kitchen. She had no desire to get in the middle of a fight.

Loud voices.

Duffy and Hank burst through the bunkhouse door. "What's happening?" Duffy asked. "Did they catch him?"

Katie shrugged. "I don't know."

The men headed for the back door. Before they could reach the hall, Lew and Brett came in holding a struggling kid. He had scraggly blond hair and a freckled face. He looked to be about twelve years old.

CHAPTER 7

"Let me go!" he cried out, jerking his arms. "I've got to go."

Using the toe of his boot to pull a chair back, Brett said, "Sit down here, son. We've got to talk to you."

The boy's dirty face had a gaunt, haggard look. His green eyes had the roving look of a caged bobcat. "Please!" he burst out. "Please, let me go!"

"Sit!" Brett pushed him into the chair. Lew moved behind the boy to hold his shoulders down.

"We're not here to hurt you, son," Brett said, moving in front of the kid. He knelt down to be at eye level with him. "You're in some kind of trouble, and we want to help you."

"Then let me go," he ground out. "Let me go now!"

Brett stood his ground. "You're not going anywhere. It's near zero out there. You'll freeze to death if the temperature dips down much more." His voice softened. "Tell us why you're out in the cold. Please believe me. We're not your enemies."

The boy looked around the room, scanning the six faces watching him. His head twitched from side to side. His face screwed up.

"What's your name?" Brett asked.

"Albie Taggart," he said, tucking his chin toward his chest.

Brett reached out and pulled a chair over. He sat in it, facing Albie knee to knee. "What happened to you? Why are you out in the cold?"

His chin quivered but his words were strong. "Ma died two weeks ago. The Widow Hazelette said we'd have to go to an orphanage." He looked up to glare at Brett, his fists clenched. "But we ain't going! Do you hear? We ain't going!"

Brett leaned toward him. "That's not what we have in mind at all, Albie. We don't want to send you to an orphanage." He slipped the next question in without a pause. "How many children are in your family?"

"Me and Jane," he said.

"How old is Jane?"

"Ten."

Katie felt a physical pain go through her.

She was just a little older than Georgina.

Albie went on without prompting, "She's sick. I tried to find some money to buy her some medicine, but I couldn't find any." Tears clouded his eyes. Angrily, he swiped at his face.

"Where is she?" Brett asked gently. "We'll bring her here where it's warm and take care of her."

Albie looked up, still afraid.

"She has to have help," Brett said. "You know she does."

Hanging his head, the boy nodded. "I'll show you where."

Brett turned to Hank. "Saddle four horses." To Duffy, "Bring me some rope," he said.

Katie gasped in alarm.

Looking at her, Brett said, "Don't worry. I'm not going to hogtie him, although I ought to." He turned to the boy. "Stand up, son. We're going to have to search you for weapons. You may just get it into your head to run off again. We can't take a chance on that."

Albie endured the humiliation with insolent patience.

Brett lifted a small knife from the boy's belt and a rope slingshot from his pocket.

"No gun?" Lew asked.

Albie looked behind him. "Pa took the Colt with him for the trail."

Brett drew up. "Where is your father then?"

"He went to find work on the railroad. Our cattle all died last summer, and Pa went out to find work. He sent us money a couple times, but then Ma got sick." His voice grew louder. "We couldn't find Pa. We didn't know where to look for him. He's going to come back to the ranch next spring, and he won't know where to find us neither!"

Brett put his hand on the boy's shoulder and stooped to look him in the eye. "We're going to help you, Albie. We'll help you find your father. Come spring you'll be able to go back home. Everything will be all right. I promise you."

Katie hoped he was right. A lot of things could happen to a man working for the railroad.

Brett glanced at his men. "Rollie and Lew, you'll come with us." He turned to Katie. "You'll have to get a bed ready for the sick child." He hesitated, thinking. "She ought to be in with you — ladies together and all that." He let out a breath as he made a decision. "We'll trade. You can take my room. It has a double bed, and you can look after the girl. I'll take your room."

Duffy returned with the rope and handed it to Brett.

Measuring off a loop, Brett went on to Katie, "It'll just be until we can make other sleeping arrangements."

He set a loop over Albie's head and worked it down to the boy's waist. "This is to keep you from running off in the dark. I'm sorry to have to do this, but I can't trust you just yet."

Sullen, the boy watched as Brett wrapped the loop around three times, tying each circlet with a separate knot. "That ought to hold you."

Katie grabbed two biscuits and handed them to the boy. His eyes lit up when he took them from her. He swallowed the first one in two gulps. The second one in three.

A few minutes later, they rode out. Duffy and Hank stayed in the kitchen to wait. Hank brought the checkerboard out, and they sat down for a game. Katie brought in the plate of stew from the box outside and returned the food to the pot. She set it on the stove to warm it up and hurried to Brett's room to get the bed ready.

Made of dark wood with four square posts and deep side rails, the bed was sturdy but not very attractive. Stripping back the covers, she wondered if Brett had made it or bought it somewhere. It had a rope-hung mattress that was stuffed with cotton, quite expensive for a frame as rough as this one was.

She stripped the bed and rolled the sheets into a bundle. Taking Brett at his word that there were no extra sheets in the house, she pulled up a quilt and smoothed it over the mattress. That would have to do until she could take care of some washing tomorrow.

Less than an hour later, Brett hello-ed the house. The men forgot their checkers game and dashed outside to help.

Katie went to the doorway and peered out. Lew had a child bundled in his arms, covered by the new army blanket Katie had set out. Lew handed the child to Duffy.

Katie stood aside so Duffy could pass her. She could see nothing of the girl as he made his way inside.

"Take her to Brett's room," she told Duffy's back.

He didn't hesitate but marched right on through. He laid her down on the bed and pulled the wool blanket back from her face. "She's burning up," he said. He touched her flushed forehead and shook his head. "It hurts a body to see a little one so stove in."

Rollie came in holding a leather satchel.

"Here are her things," he said.

Jane Taggart had thick black hair done up in two wide, frazzled braids. She had soft, curving cheeks with her dark lashes forming perfect half moons across them.

Her eyes stayed closed while Katie undressed her and slipped the nightgown on her that had been in her bag. The child was starved. Somehow, Katie had to figure out how to get some nourishment into her.

Pulling the quilts around the girl's chin, Katie hurried to the kitchen. Someone had dished up a bowl of stew for Albie. The boy was sitting at the table, shoveling food into his mouth. Poor kids. How had they survived at all?

Pulling a small pot from under the counter, Katie spooned some stew into it and added water. She poked and stirred the meat until it fell to bits and mashed the potatoes until she had a slightly lumpy broth. "I'm going to need some help," she said to no one in particular as she poured a glass of water.

Without a word, Brett stood up and followed her into the bedroom.

"We've got to wake her up enough to eat a little," Katie told him. "Can you help her sit up while I try to feed her some of this? The last thing we need is for her to choke."

"Poor tyke," he said. He sat on the edge of the bed and slid his arm under the child's frail shoulders. "Come on, honey. Let's wake up." He gently shook her chin. "Wake up, Jane. Can you hear me?"

Jane's eyelid's fluttered. She let out a pouty moan.

Katie leaned in closer to speak directly into the girl's face. "Open your mouth, Jane. Eat." She held the bowl close to her face. "Smell that?"

The beefy aroma brought her around. She had large brown eyes, unfocused but obviously very aware of the stew. She opened her mouth, and Katie put a small spoonful on her tongue. She swallowed and opened for another until half the bowl had disappeared.

"Water," she said, her tongue thick.

Jane set down the bowl and held the glass to Jane's peeling lips. She swallowed three times, then relaxed.

"Let her rest now," Katie told Brett. She backed away to give him room to move off the bed and lay Jane back on the pillow. Carefully covering her, Brett stood watching Jane breathe for a few seconds.

Katie whispered, "Pray for her, will you, please?"

He glanced at Katie and for a moment

she almost expected him to reach for her hand. But he didn't. He simply bowed and said, "Lord, we thank You for helping us find these poor children. We place them in Your care. Give Jane strength. Please help her to get well."

With that they tiptoed from the room.

Outside the bedroom door, Brett stopped to say, "We're putting Albie in the bunkhouse. He needs a bath in the worst way, but we'll take care of that later. I don't think the boy could stand anything more tonight. He's almost as done in as Jane."

Katie said, "I'll look after them in the morning."

He rubbed his jaw. "I guess they'll have to stay here until spring. I don't see any other way about it. We can't send them back to their ranch alone, and that widow woman isn't going to send them away, that's for sure."

Katie pressed her lips into a soft upside-down smile. "You're a good man, Brett," she murmured.

He grinned. "It's nice to hear you say so. I think you're fine yourself."

She stepped back to break the spell. "I'd best get some things from my room," she said.

Still watching her with that light in his

eyes, he nodded. "You'd better do that."

She hurried away like a kid running from a brush fire when the wind had come up and blown sparks everywhere. If she wasn't careful, she'd get herself singed.

The next few days were a whirlwind of activity for Katie. She lost two nights of sleep tending to Jane. She washed sheets and scrubbed the children's filthy clothes. She cooked massive meals and watched Albie eat enough for two men.

Before dawn on the third morning, Katie woke up to find Jane lying in sheets soaked with sweat, her dark hair matted to her head. She was shivering.

Rushing for her own extra nightgown, Katie got the child changed and pulled off the sheets for washing yet again. When she had her comfortable, Katie brought her some soup and watched her feed herself.

"Your fever has broken. You're going to get better," she told the child. "Albie will be so happy when he wakes up this morning. I'll tell him he can come in and see you."

"Is Albie all right?" Jane murmured. "He's not sick, is he?" She had wide brown eyes that looked so helpless.

Katie took the empty bowl from her. "He's right as rain, Jane," she said in a singsong. "He'll come to see you in the morning without warning."

Jane smiled wearily, her eyes already drooping.

Katie set the bowl on the dresser and slid between the covers next to the child. She snuggled deeper into the pillow and fell asleep before she'd taken two breaths.

The next thing she knew, light was streaming through the window. She blinked and sat up. What on earth? She was so late for breakfast that the men had probably gone without eating. Why hadn't someone knocked on the door?

She flipped the covers back and pulled her brown skirt over her nightgown, topping it with a navy shirtwaist. Not waiting for her shoes, she scurried to the kitchen. It was empty. The biscuit tin was empty, too, and the coffeepot sat on the stove, about one-third full.

The bunkhouse door was open. Stepping over to close it, she caught sight of Albie sound asleep, his mouth open and one arm flung over his head. He was an attractive child when his defenses were down.

She gently closed the door and headed toward Brett's bedroom to dress properly. Before she reached the sitting-room door, he came in. She touched her hair. She'd totally forgotten to comb it.

He grinned when he saw her. "So there you are. I thought you might sleep till noon."

"What time is it?" she asked.

He pulled his pocket watch from his pants pocket and looked at it. "Seven-thirty."

She yawned and covered her mouth. "Jane's fever broke sometime before dawn. I had to change the bed and her, too. I warmed some soup for her and she ate all of it. She's sleeping now."

"Why don't you head back to bed, too?" he asked. "You're all in."

She frowned. "I've got to see to lunch."

"We'll eat biscuit-and-bacon sandwiches today. The men completely understand." His smile was soft and warm. "Go ahead. Sleep while those kids are snoozing. It'll do you good."

Her eyes did feel heavy. Maybe she could close them for just a few minutes. "All right," she said.

He patted his pockets. "Now why did I come in here? I was after something." Frowning, he stared at the plank floor. Finally, he shook his head. "Oh well, it'll come to me. I'll be back in a few minutes when it does." He grinned at her. "Katie, I'd be tempted to say you've driven every thought from my head." Chuckling at her shocked expression, he turned and went out.

CHAPTER 8

With the resilience of a child's constitution, within three days Jane and Albie had life in their eyes again. After three weeks no one would have known the ordeal they'd just come through, if it weren't for Jane's occasional nightmares.

Without being asked, Albie went to the barn with the men to help with the chores. He split wood for Katie and gathered the eggs. In the evenings, Lew and Duffy took turns playing checkers with Albie and teaching him their wily ways at the board. Jane loved to watch them and offer her brother her own brand of advice.

"How did you manage to come and go around here without leaving any tracks?" Lew asked Albie one evening over the checkerboard.

"My pa taught me to track," the boy said. He jumped two of Lew's men. "I wrapped my shoes in burlap whenever I left our camp, and I stayed out of the brush as much as I could so I wouldn't break no branches."

Lew made a move. "Sounds like you could teach me a thing or two," he said. "We'll go hunting later in the week. How about that?"

The boy brightened. "Sure," he said. "Can I carry a Winchester?"

Lew chuckled at his sudden enthusiasm. "We'll see about that," he said.

The next morning, Jane watched Katie patting doughy globs into perfect circles at the worktable. "Can I help you make biscuits?" she asked. The top of the girl's head almost reached Katie's shoulder.

"I don't see why not," Katie replied, her hands still in motion. "Wash your hands, and I'll show you how."

Jane skipped to the pump and dipped her fingers in the washbasin. Drying her hands on the towel there, she came back.

Using her chin, Katie pointed toward the bank of cabinets. "There's an apron in the second door on the bottom."

Jane found the bleached bit of muslin and wrapped it around her waist. "Ma showed me how to do this," she said, a hint of pride in her voice. She wrapped the strings around her waist and wound them to the front where she tied a bow. "I used to help her with biscuits, too."

Katie moved the bowl of flour so it sat between them on the worktable. "This is the way I do it," she said. She dropped a spoonful of flour into her palm, scooped an egg-sized lump of dough on top of that with more flour on top, then she flipped the dough between both hands, shaping it into a smooth circle. She dropped it onto the half-filled pan and said, "Let's see you do it now, Jane."

With nimble fingers, Jane imitated Katie's actions perfectly. Her finished biscuit wasn't quite as smooth as Katie's, but it came close.

"That's excellent!" Katie exclaimed. "I can see you're going to be a big help around here."

Jane smiled with satisfaction. "Ma always let me help her." Suddenly, her smile faded. Her mouth tightened and she lowered her chin. She kept making biscuits, but she didn't talk anymore.

Katie wanted to pull the girl into her arms, but she didn't think Jane would respond to her in that way. Instead, she gave her some quiet and some space for her thoughts. If only they could help the children reunite with their father. There had to be a way to find him.

That evening at supper, Brett said, "We

need to make a trip to town sometime in the next week. It'll be Christmas in a few days. I'd like to get some fixin's for a nice Christmas dinner." He glanced at Katie at the other end of the table. "That is, if you'd like to."

Katie smiled at Jane sitting in the once-empty seat between her and Rollie. "That would be fun, wouldn't it? We may be able to make some molasses cookies."

"Gingerbread men!" Jane said, her face shining. "We make those every year."

Katie raised her eyebrows and looked at Brett. "Gingerbread men," she said. Her eyes thanked him in a way that words could have never done.

He sent her that small smile and something inside her felt warm.

He looked at Duffy. "You're the one that's always looking at the sky. What's the weather sizing up to be?"

"Not a cloud in sight," the old-timer said. He dipped the edge of his biscuit in molasses. "Besides the burning cold, there's no bad weather heading our way that I can see. But that could change any minute. You know that."

Brett said, "Town's only a little over an hour's ride from here. Let's go tomorrow morning." He looked around the table. "It'll be a cold trip. Who wants to come along?"

After a long moment of silence, Katie said, "I would, if you don't mind."

"I'll go," Hank said.

Brett nodded. "That'll make three of us, then."

Katie added, "I'll set food on the back of the stove for those who stay."

"If we leave at daybreak, we should be back by noon," Brett said. He looked at Albie. "Take care of your sister while we're gone, son. And keep the fires stoked."

The boy nodded.

While Albie and Jane washed the supper dishes, Katie pulled out her stash of money, now hidden inside her pillowcase. She had twenty dollars saved from her cleaning money. She would buy some presents and send a package to Ma and the kids, something for Jane, too. Katie figured Albie was too man-grown even at twelve to appreciate a present from her when none of the hands were getting anything. She couldn't afford to buy a gift for everyone in the house. But something for Jane, definitely.

Tingling with excitement, she dropped the coins into her coat pocket and returned to the kitchen. She had to get beans ready for cooking. That was something even Duffy could heat up for lunch tomorrow in case they were delayed in getting back.

The morning was bitter cold, much colder than Katie's trip to the ranch almost three months before. She dressed in her warmest clothes, three layers deep with her coat over all.

When she reached the kitchen, Brett handed her a pair of cowboy boots and two pairs of wool socks. "Take off your shoes and put these on," he told her. "You can carry the shoes with you to wear while you're in town. Your feet will freeze otherwise."

"Thanks. I'll have to get my buttonhook." She set the boots near the table and quickly returned. When she finished unbuttoning her shoes, she slid the buttonhook into her coat pocket. The socks and heavy boots forced her to walk stiff-legged to keep from falling.

Brett held her arms to steady her on the kitchen stoop, then gave her a leg up into the saddle. When she was settled, he handed her a bear rug. "Wrap this around you to keep your face from freezing," he told her.

Huddled in the saddle, she felt like a furry package, but she was definitely warmer than she had been on her ride into the Masten Ranch last October.

They arrived in Rosita shortly after nine

o'clock. A one-street town with a dirt thoroughfare, the main shopping center had two stores — an emporium and a milliner's shop. Brett helped Katie down and supported her into the emporium where a giant potbelly stove had four chairs pulled near it. She gratefully sank into a chair, closing her teary eyes and breathing in the warm air.

"Do you have some hot coffee?" Brett asked the storekeeper.

Within minutes a steaming cup nestled between Katie's hands. Every sip was heavenly. "I'm afraid we'll have to wait awhile before we can head back," she told Brett sitting across from her. Hank had taken the horses to the livery stable, then set out to find his own diversion.

"You've got all the time you need," he said gently. "The men lived without a cook for six weeks. They'll make it through the day without you."

She grinned, and her lips felt stiff. "They won't like it."

He smirked. "They'll survive."

When her hands thawed enough to manipulate the buttonhook, Brett helped her slide out of the boots, and she put on her shoes. "That's better," she said, standing and flexing her toes. "I almost feel human again."

Brett approached the counter where the shopkeeper waited. He was a tall balding man with bulging eyes. Permanently bent, his narrow back joined his long neck, forming a smooth arc that ended at the crown of his head. With his head permanently bent forward, he looked upward at Brett with those big eyes in an expression that seemed grotesque. "How can I help you, Mr. Masten?" he asked, his voice surprisingly smooth.

Brett said, "Mr. Sullivan, this is my new cook, Katie Priestly. She'll tell you what she needs for the ranch. Please, put everything on my bill. I'll be back with a pack horse in a few minutes."

Sullivan nodded and his whole upper body weaved. He hooked his thumbs beneath his black suspenders. "What can I get for you, little lady?"

Katie handed him the list she'd written the night before. "I've got some personal shopping to do as well," she said.

"I'll be back shortly," Brett said, heading for the door.

Katie took her time, letting her body soak in the warmth of the store while she browsed among the goods. Sullivan carried everything from canned goods to dried fruit, from bolts of fabric to kitchen wares. He sold lamps and carpets, seeds and garden tools.

She chose peppermint sticks for the children, six in all. She figured Albie wasn't so old that he'd be insulted by a piece of candy. She bought three books of paper dolls as well, figuring those would be easy to mail to her littler sisters, and Jane would like them, too. A pair of white gloves for Bonnie, a snap-brim hat for Mark, and four yards of fine calico fabric for Ma.

She was handing the fabric bolt to Mr. Sullivan for cutting when Brett strode in. He held an envelope in his hand.

"This came for you," he said.

He handed her a letter addressed in Bonnie's handwriting. Concern creased Katie's face. Ma was usually the one to write on the envelope.

Moving to a chair near the stove, she tore it open and scanned the message inside.

Dear Katie,
  Ma is sick. She has a fever and hasn't eaten for two days. Georgina and Arlene are crying. I wish you were here.
                              Love,
                              Bonnie

She handed the letter to Brett.

He read it and handed it back. "How old is Bonnie?" he asked.

"Thirteen."

"Is she the oldest at home?"

Katie nodded.

"You'll have to go," he said with conviction. "I'll go with you."

"Just like that? What about the hands? What about Albie and Jane?"

"Let's take the children with us. The men can fend for themselves." He stepped up to the counter. "Mr. Sullivan, add two sides of bacon to that order, will you please? And we'll need those things wrapped up right away."

He moved to Katie's side and said, "Can you get those boots back on okay? I'm going to round up Hank and fetch the pack horse."

When she nodded, Brett headed out.

She unbuttoned her shoes with the methodical ease that comes with practice. She wouldn't have to mail those Christmas presents after all. But she hated the thought of leaving Rollie, Hank, Duffy, and Lew alone without a decent meal until she returned. There wasn't time for her to do much extra cooking for them either.

She pushed her padded feet into the

116

boots. How in the world would they be able to get all the way home in this cold without freezing in the process?

As an afterthought, she picked up two pairs of leather gloves, one for Johnny and one for Pa. Neither of them would probably be there while she was at home, but she could save them for spring when she saw them again.

Twenty minutes later, Brett helped her mount up, and they headed home. Pushing the horses to their top speed for the distance, they reached the ranch yard in less than an hour. Brett led the horses to the porch stoop and swung down to help Katie. He handed the reins to Hank, who took the two saddled horses to the barn while Brett unloaded the pack horse.

As soon as Katie entered the house, Albie shoved his arms into his coat sleeves and strode out to help Brett carry in the goods. Jane was at the table, the checkerboard in front of her, when Katie came in.

"Jane," she said, "we came back early. I got some bad news from home."

Jane stood up. "What is it?"

"My mother is sick," Katie said. "She has a fever."

A look of horror crossed Jane's small face. She ran to Katie and threw her arms around her waist.

Katie leaned over to hug the child. "I'm going to her," she said into Jane's ear. "I want you and Albie to come with me. Do you want to?"

Jane nodded. She drew away and wiped her wet cheeks, sniffling. "When do we go?"

"First thing in the morning." Katie pulled off her coat and scarf. "We have so much to do. I'll need your help."

"We have to make biscuits," Jane said. "Lots of them."

Katie chuckled at the girl's unexpected insight.

"I can do it if you measure everything," Jane said.

Katie caressed the top of the child's dark hair. "You're a good girl, Jane. That would help me a lot."

She sat down to get out of those boots.

Brett and Albie came in with the goods from town, then left for the barn on some errand while Brett explained their plans to the boy.

Wearing her own shoes, Katie carried her things to Brett's bedroom. When she returned, Jane had everything on the worktable: flour, lard, salt, baking soda, and a large bowl.

Katie bent over to pull a wide, flat pan

from the cabinet. "We'll need a lot of them, Janey, my girl — some for us to take on the trail and some to leave with the hands. If we set some biscuits outside in that box, they'll freeze for later. We can put a pot of beans out there, too. In that way, it's good to have it cold outside."

"We already have a pot of beans," Jane said, looking at their lunch that was still on the stove.

Katie reached for another bowl. "While you're doing that, I'll make cornbread, too.

When Albie came in, Katie had him bring in a haunch of beef for stewing and then she put him to slicing bacon with her sharpest knife.

She stayed so busy that she hardly had time to think of the trip. It was almost nine o'clock that evening when she finally packed her saddlebags. She had helped Jane pack her things after supper and then had sent the girl to bed, worried about her and the cold day to follow.

They ate a quick breakfast, preparing to leave shortly before dawn. Katie stepped outside and drew up, surprised.

Brett had the buckboard pulled near the steps, the back piled high with cowhide rugs and buffalo robes. "We put in three foot warmers with hot coals in them, two in the back and one in the front," he said. "That should keep us from freezing until we get to Musgrove. Mrs. Sanford at the general store will give us some fresh coals for the rest of the trip."

He helped her in. "We should be at the ranch by nightfall if all goes well."

Relieved beyond belief, Katie leaned on his arm and climbed aboard. Jane and Albie climbed in the back and immediately set about making a nest for themselves.

Jane looked up at Katie. "We can put the stew next to the foot warmer to keep it from freezing, can't we?"

Katie nodded, smiling. "That's a wonderful idea."

"Would you rather be in back with the children?" Brett asked when he climbed aboard. "You'd be warmer there."

She shook her head. "I'll ride with you for a while," she said. "If I get cold, I'll move back."

He grinned and shook the reins. With only one foot warmer between them, they had to sit close together.

Katie looked back to see that Albie and Jane had completely buried themselves. Giggles and squirms lasted for a few minutes, then they were quiet. "They're asleep," Katie said.

"Oh, to be a child again," Brett said, glancing back.

"They've had their share of hardship," Katie reminded him.

"But they came through it like soldiers," he said. "They're good kids. I hope I have some like them one of these days."

Now that they were on their way, Katie's mind turned toward home. She missed Bonnie, Mark, Georgina, and Arlene something awful. Not to mention Johnny and Ma and Pa. She could hardly wait to hug them all.

Glancing at Brett, she felt a cold knot forming in her chest. The truth was sure to come out before this day was over. The best thing for her to do was tell him now.

CHAPTER 9

Unfortunately, making that decision was a thousand times easier than carrying it out. Musgrove appeared in the valley below them, and Katie hadn't said a single word about her falsehood. Several times she'd opened her mouth to speak, but the words wouldn't come. Brett was a good and honest man. He would surely scorn her when she told him.

But Johnny would give her away. He would run out to greet her and call her "sis" like he always did. She had to tell Brett herself before that happened.

"Brett . . ."

He leaned toward her, bending his head sideways. "Yes?"

"I have to tell you something." She shifted her feet trying to catch some last ray of warmth from the foot warmer.

"Did I ever tell you about the time my brother fell in the well?" he said. Without waiting for her to reply, he started into the story. Katie glanced back to see Albie and Jane with their noses uncovered, listening to Brett's tale. How could she stop him now?

With growing misery, she watched the shanty town of Musgrove come closer and closer with the resigned dread of a convicted felon on his way to the gallows.

They reached the general store, and the children hopped down from the back of the wagon.

Katie eyed the door, sure that Johnny would appear at any moment. When he didn't she grew worried.

Brett didn't seem to notice her discomfort. He handed her down and led the horse to the watering trough, now topped by a layer of ice. He had to break through it for the horse to drink.

Katie hurried inside. "Hello, Mrs. Sanford," she said, anxiously. "Where's Johnny?"

The old woman shook her head. "He got word that his mother was sick, so he lit out day before yesterday." She peered at Katie. "Aren't you his sister?"

With a furtive glance at the children eyeing the candy jar, Katie quickly nodded. "I'm going home as well," she said, keeping her voice quiet. "We stopped to see if we can get something to drink and some hot coals for our foot warmers."

Mrs. Sullivan nodded. "I've got coffee on the stove," she said. "Coals are ten cents a shovelful."

Brett stepped inside at her last words. He carried the foot warmers in his hands with several small blankets over his arm. "We sure do appreciate the coffee," he said. "I hate to be a bother, but can you put about half milk in the children's cups?"

"It's no bother." Mrs. Sullivan bustled about filling the order while Brett and Katie sat near the fire.

"My face is cold," she told him, rubbing her mittens over her cheeks.

"How long did it take for you to get here from the ranch last October?" he asked her.

She held her hands toward the stove. "We left before noon and didn't get here until suppertime. But we had to stop every little while to warm up. My feet almost froze because I didn't have proper boots. That made the trip twice as long as it should have been."

He nodded. "I'm hoping we can make it there in a couple more hours. Even with the foot warmers, it's going to get cold before we reach the ranch. We may have to stop and build a fire."

They lingered at the general store for an hour to let their limbs warm up, then they set off again. Buried under their rugs, Albie and Jane's voices drifted upward, too muffled to understand their meaning. From time to time a single word like pa or ma would burst up like popcorn out of a roasting basket.

When Musgrove disappeared behind them, Katie said, "Brett, I must speak to you about something."

He pulled the buffalo robe further down over her face. "Lean on me," he said. "You'll stay warmer." He put his arm about her shoulders, and she naturally slid closer. The shoulder of his buffalo coat felt so warm under her cheek. "Don't worry yourself, Katie," he murmured. "Everything is going to be all right."

He went on, "Tell me, what do you think of my house? It's an odd setup having the bunkhouse attached, I know."

"It's a great setup," she said. "The hands don't have to go outside for their meals, but you still have the privacy of your own place. I think it's fine."

"It's rough," he said.

She chuckled. "You could use some curtains" — her eyes drifted closed — "and a rug or two, maybe some padded furniture . . ."

The next thing she knew, he was shaking her awake. "Wake up, Katie. We've got to stop and build a fire. I was hoping we wouldn't have to, but my feet are like ice. I know the children must be cold, too."

Blinking, she pulled the buffalo robe off and shuddered at the cold blast that hit her cheeks. She looked around. "I know this place," she said. "It's about an hour from our house." She shivered. "Can we make it that far?"

Brett turned to call to the children. "Albie! Jane!"

Albie pulled the cowhide rug away from his face and looked at Brett.

"Are you freezing back there?" Brett asked him.

His chin quivered as he said, "Jane's really cold."

"We'll try to find some shelter and build a fire. If we can put some coals in these foot warmers, we can make it the rest of the way without any problem."

Katie squinted at the landscape. "There are two big rocks with a hollowed out place between them. They're somewhere near here." Suddenly, she pointed. "There! See them?" Orange-red and jutting up fifteen feet into the air, the boulders stood shoulder to shoulder a hundred yards ahead.

The wagon rumbled over the rough ground as Brett edged closer and closer to the crack between the rocks. "We need to get the horses as close in as we can to shelter them from the wind," he said.

"There's no water here," Katie told him when he set the brake.

"We'll manage," he replied, helping her down.

The children scrambled out of the wagon and began to search for wood. Katie went into the rocky shelter. Someone had been there recently. They'd kicked apart a half-burned fire. She knelt to rebuild it with the charred sticks. They would light much faster than fresh branches.

A few minutes later, Brett and the children came in with their arms loaded. Albie broke the smaller branches over his knee and made a small pile of them. Using his knife, Brett shaved a couple of dry sticks into tinder and pulled a small tin of matches from his pocket.

The fire caught on the first match and quickly grew.

"That was a blessing, having the wood already here," Brett said. "Let's gather around and pray for a safe journey the rest of the way, shall we?" The four of them circled the small fire and joined hands. Brett prayed a simple prayer, and peace settled over them. Albie lay on his side, propped up on one elbow. Jane sat with her boots near the fire, her knees bent with her chin resting on them.

Feeding the flames, Brett said, "Does anyone want to know why Duffy's horse has a bell?"

Katie smiled. "Is this another joke?"

He laughed. "No. Actually, it's the real reason. I figured now that we're away from the likes of Rollie and Hank, I could tell you the truth about that."

"What is it?" Katie asked.

He dropped a stick on the fire. "Have you ever heard of a bell mare?"

Albie said, "I have."

Brett grinned at him. "Go ahead, Albie. Tell her what it is."

The boy said, "It's a mare that keeps the horses in a remuda together. She has a bell on her and the horses stay near that sound. When the horse wrangler wants to find the remuda, he listens for the bell."

Brett grinned. "That's it. We run both longhorns and horses. Duffy uses the bell to keep our string of horses together on the range. It's amazing how they follow him around like little puppy dogs. He's a first-rate wrangler." He peered into the flames. "It looks like we've got some good coals brewing in there."

While they waited for the coals to multiply, Katie told the children, "I can't wait for you to meet the kids at the Priestly house. There are three girls and a boy your age, Albie. His name is Mark."

"How old are the girls?" Jane asked, tilting her head. Her top lip formed a perfect bow shape.

"Bonnie is the oldest. She's thirteen. Then there's Georgina. She's nine, and Arlene is five. Georgina has pigtails just like yours except they're a little lighter brown than yours. She's full of fun. I know you'll love to play with her."

Jane's face glowed with anticipation. "I always wanted a sister," she said, "but Ma said the Lord didn't will it."

Albie let out a grunt. "Me neither," he said, dropping a small stick on the fire.

Jane went on. "Ma was always sickly. She said she was glad she had the two of us. That was a miracle."

"You'll like Mark," Katie told Albie. "He loves horses and hunting."

Albie rested his chin on his hand and gazed into the fire. Jane chattered about Molly Chambers, her best friend at school.

Half an hour later, they were snug in the wagon and heading down the trail. They reached the ranch around noon.

The Tumbling P was a small affair, about half the size of the Masten Ranch. The house was a square cabin with three dormers coming out from the front of the roof. Those dormers shed light on the children's domain. As they entered the small yard, Katie looked up and saw a pixie face in the window of the center dormer. It immediately disappeared.

Beyond the house, the remains of the barn lay as charred and bleak as the Priestly family's current prospects. Katie's heart pounded in her ears. The family would begin pouring out to greet them. One of them would surely give her away. Why hadn't she told Brett the truth when she had the chance?

Still shrugging into his coat, Johnny was the first one to appear. He paused on the steps to gaze at the group, wondering who they were. Then he spotted Katie and ran toward her. She leaned over the side of the wagon for him to lift her down.

"Katie!" he cried, welcoming her into his arms. "It's so good to see you! We didn't think you'd be able to come."

She threw her arms tightly around his

neck and hugged him hard. "Don't call me sis," she whispered into his ear. "Do you hear me?"

Puzzled, he tried to draw back and look into her eyes.

She hugged him all the harder. "Just don't call me sis, Johnny." With that she let him go and turned to hug Bonnie, who was at her elbow, and Georgina next to her.

Finally remembering her manners, Katie waved her hand toward the wagon seat and said, "Meet Brett Masten. He was kind enough to bring me here when he heard Ma was sick."

The Taggart children had already climbed down from the wagon and were standing shyly near Katie's back.

"Albie and Jane Taggart," Katie went on. She turned to Georgina. "Jane is about your age, Georgina. Why don't you take her inside and see if you can find something fun to do?" The girls looked into each others' eyes, giggled, and ran for the house. Two sets of pigtails bounced with each stride.

To Albie, Katie said, "Mark will show you where to put your things."

"Let's go inside," Bonnie said, shivering. She looked very like Katie except her features were smaller. They had the same brown eyes and fair skin, the same wavy dark hair.

Bonnie linked arms with Katie and rested her head on Katie's shoulder. "I'm so glad to see you I could just cry."

"How is Mother?" Katie asked, loosening her arm to slip it around her sister's waist.

"She's better, thank the Lord," Bonnie replied as they crossed the threshold into the kitchen. It had a warm smell from bubbling chicken soup.

Like the Masten place, the Priestlys' kitchen was in front and to the left of the door. The dining area was to the right. With a sofa pushed against the far wall, it doubled as a sitting room.

Bonnie went on. "Mrs. Andrews came and helped us. She stayed for two days. Ma started getting better right away. I don't know what we would have done without her, Katie." Strain still showed on the girl's face.

Katie hugged her. "It's over now." She rested her cheek against Bonnie's for a second. "We have *so much* to be thankful for. I'll tell you all about it later." She turned loose of her sister to unbutton her coat. Laughing, she said, "I've got to get out of these boots first thing or I'll fall over."

From behind her, Brett said, "I brought

your shoes in."

Katie turned to beam at him. "Thank you. I forgot them. I guess I'm a little excited." She sat in a chair at the table to kick off the boots. "I want to go in and see Ma before I button those things on. They take too long."

At that moment, a short, thin man came from the back room. He had thinning gray hair and papery cheeks.

Katie gasped. "Pa!" She lunged up to run to him and almost fell. She still had one boot on.

Brett jumped forward to catch her.

With a little shriek she clung to him. "I'm all right," she said, laughing. "Help me off with this boot!"

He knelt to pull it off.

Once she was free, she skipped into her father's arms. His face was thin, but he had a smile in his hazel eyes. "Katie, girl!" He stroked her hair.

"When did you come home?" she asked. She couldn't stop smiling.

"Yesterday. I had the chance to take off a week for the Christmas holiday, so I took it. Bonnie had sent me word that Ma was sick. I had to come." He turned and put his arm about Katie's shoulders. "She wants to see you."

They entered her parents' room, and

133

Johnny came in after them. On the bed, Ma looked so weak. Her dark hair was sprinkled with gray, and her skin looked pasty.

"Katie!" she breathed. "I'm so glad to see you." She raised her hand to touch her daughter's face.

Katie bent over to kiss her fragile cheek. Sitting on the edge of the bed, Katie said, "How are you feeling?"

The sick woman's voice was breathy. "I'm tired, but I'm going to be all right. I get stronger every day."

They talked for a few moments then Katie turned to her brother. "Johnny, would you please close the door. I have something to tell all of you."

CHAPTER 10

When she finished with her story, her father said, "Katie, I have to ask you something, and I want you to tell me the truth." He had a set look on his face that she recognized. There would be no weaseling out of anything.

"Of course."

"I saw you with him just now," he said, his hazel eyes keen as he looked at her. "What's between the two of you?"

Katie looked sheepish. "It's a big muddle, Pa," she said. "He's a fine Christian man, and I'd give anything to have him ask me to marry him."

"Do you love him, honey?" Ma asked.

Katie nodded. "But he thinks I'm married to Johnny. If I tell him I'm not, what does that make me?" She sighed.

Johnny scowled. "I can't believe you did that, sis! That puts me in a bad position, too."

Pa said, "Well, Katie's going to have to set him straight. It's not right to let the lie stand, child. You know that."

She nodded. "I'll tell him myself. Before we leave here, I'll tell him." She squeezed her mother's hand. "I may have to stay here with you after that."

"And welcome," Ma said, lifting Katie's hand to her lips. She let her hand fall back to the quilt. "I need to rest now."

The three of them left the room and softly closed the door.

In the dining room, Bonnie was skipping around setting bowls on the table.

Looking at all of them gathered there, Johnny said, "Tomorrow's Christmas Eve. Let's make this a special Christmas!"

He said to Brett, "Would you come with me to cut a tree? I know of one not far from here that would be perfect for that corner." He nodded toward an empty nook beside the sofa. "Mark and Albie, too."

Brett gave that small smile. "I'm game."

The boys looked interested.

Johnny picked up the coffeepot. "Who wants coffee?" he asked, lifting an enamel cup from the counter. He filled three mugs then lifted a jug of milk to fill several glasses.

"Let's make Christmas cookies," Georgina said, sharing a smile with Jane.

Katie sat at the table near the girls. "We've got one whole day to get ready," she said. "Let's make a battle plan."

Everyone gathered around the long table — the six Priestly children, Albie and Jane, Brett, and even Pa. He sat at the head of the table and watched them talking as though he couldn't get enough of looking at them all.

As they ate lunch and discussed Christmas fun, Katie had the strange feeling that she was watching herself from a corner of the room.

Eleven weeks ago she had left this house hungry and more discouraged than she could even describe. Today they were all together again, warm and fed, everyone talking at once about a happy holiday.

An hour later, they split up and set about their assigned tasks. Bonnie peeled sweet potatoes to make some pies. Katie supervised the cookie makers: Georgina, Jane, and Arlene. Mark and Albie headed outdoors with Johnny and Brett in search of a Christmas tree.

When Ma woke up from her rest, Katie took her a bowl of soup and told her of their progress. Pulling herself into a sitting position at the head of the bed, the older woman said, "Look in my sewing basket. I believe I have some white ribbon you could use to make bows for the tree."

She slowly ate the soup while Katie dug around to find the ribbon. "Here it is!" she cried, holding it up.

Ma handed Katie her bowl. "I'm so glad you're home, dear. All this excitement will do the kids so much good. This house has been too quiet for them."

Katie kissed her mother's forehead. "They've been awful worried about you, Ma. Sleep now. I'll try to keep the noise down."

Her mother smiled and reached out to catch Katie's hand. "Let them make all the noise they want," she said. "It does me good to hear them happy."

The rest of the day was a blur in Katie's mind. She laughed at Johnny's foolishness and giggled at Georgina's antics. It was so good to be home.

Always on the alert for a chance to speak to Brett alone, she hardly saw him. It seemed he was always with Johnny or else sitting with her father discussing ranching, the anthrax epidemic, or life in general.

That evening Ma was able to sit in a chair and eat her dinner. Katie sat with her and later helped her into bed. As Katie was fixing the quilt around her, Ma said, "He's a nice young man. I can see why you like him." She winked. "I'll tell you a secret. Your father likes him, too. I can tell by the way they talk to each other."

"Do you think so, Ma?" Katie said. "I haven't had a chance to tell Brett the truth yet. I've been watching for a chance, but he's always with someone." She picked up Ma's empty dishes and returned to the kitchen.

The Christmas tree stood in the designated corner, slightly bent at the top but otherwise beautiful with its popcorn garland and white bows.

All the children slept in the second-floor loft — one huge room with a blanket hung down the center of it. Boys on the right and girls on the left of that "Mason-Dixon Line." Two wide beds stood on each side, all piled high with quilts and comforters. Since Georgina and Jane wanted to be together, all three girls filled up one bed. Katie was alone in the other one.

She had a difficult time getting the three youngest girls to bed on Christmas Eve. They wanted to chase each other and giggle. Once she even caught them jumping on their bed.

"What are you doing?" she demanded in a hoarse whisper. "If Pa hears you jumping up here, he'll come up!"

The giggles stopped and finally they settled down. Kissing each of them, Katie found the package she'd hidden in her saddlebags and carried it downstairs. Without opening it, she laid the entire thing under the Christmas tree.

As usual, Brett was talking to Pa — Brett at the dining table and Pa sitting in a corner of the sofa. Albie and Mark were playing checkers at the other end of the table with Bonnie looking on. Johnny came down from the loft and sat beside Katie, who was at the table near her father.

"Since you work for the railroad," Brett was saying to Pa, "I was hoping you might know how to find their father. His name is Rudolph Taggart."

"I'll certainly do what I can," Pa said. "As soon as I get back, I'll ask at the office. They must have a way to track people down."

Mark spoke up for the first time. "Why can't they stay here until their pa comes back?" he said. "We have enough to eat now. Why can't they stay?"

Katie looked at Brett. From the expression on his face she knew he was waiting for her to speak.

"What do you think?" she asked Pa.

He nodded. "I don't see why not. Albie

would give Mark some company. He has a lot on him keeping the wood box filled and the chores done."

"Jane's handy in the kitchen," Katie told Bonnie. "She's been a big help to me." She smiled at Brett. "I'd miss them."

His smile was slow and warm. "I'd miss them, too. On the other hand, they'd be happier here with the other children. Don't you think so?"

She nodded. "You're right. It's for the best. If Pa finds Mr. Taggart, he could bring him back here to fetch Albie and Jane home. It would be a lot easier that way." She looked at Albie. "What do you want to do? Would you mind staying?"

He shrugged. "I wouldn't mind staying," he said. He moved a checker piece. "Jane likes playing with the girls, too."

"It would only be about three months," Katie told him. "If you change your mind and you'd rather come back to stay with us, send a letter and we'll come and get you." She looked at Brett for confirmation and he nodded.

Johnny yawned. "It's been a long day. I'm going to turn in," he said. He patted Katie's shoulder. "Good night, everyone."

Pa stood up. "I'll stoke the fire."

Brett held up his hand. "I'll take care of

that for you, Mr. Priestly," he said.

"Why, thank you, Brett. That's good of you." He touched Katie's hair. "Good night."

Brett left the room to pile wood into two stoves: the kitchen cook stove and the potbelly stove in the dead center of the room.

The boys finished their game, and the three older children went upstairs as well.

Brett clanked the last iron door closed and stood, dusting off his hands. He moved to the washbasin to rinse away traces of soot from his fingers.

"You have a nice family," he said, drying his hands. He looked directly at her, his eyes calm but also full of purpose.

Katie felt a lump forming in her throat.

He flipped the towel over its rack and sat next to her at the table.

"I've been trying to tell you something," she managed at last.

"But I wouldn't let you," he said.

She looked up at him, a frown between her eyes.

He leaned closer. "I wouldn't let you," he said more forcefully, "for a reason."

"Brett, I'm not married." The words burst out before she'd fully formed them in her mind. "I lied to you."

He clasped her hand and lifted it to his lips. She gazed into his eyes and couldn't look away.

"You may have lied to me," he said, his words soft and gentle, "but you didn't fool me. Not for a minute."

"You knew all along?" she gasped. "Why did you hire me then?"

He kissed her fingers. "Because you were desperate. I could see it all over you. I could also see that you weren't used to telling stories. It was eating you up. It still is." He grew serious. "I wanted to help you more than anything," he said, "but I was in a tough spot, too."

She nodded. "The more I got to know the men, the more I could see why you made that rule. The entire atmosphere of the ranch would have been different if any of the men were competing for my attention." She lowered her chin. "Not that they would have."

He lifted her chin so he could look into her eyes. "Don't kid yourself. Every one of the hands is half in love with you."

"They are?" She forgot to breathe.

He nodded. "All but me." He leaned even closer. "I'm not half in love with you, Katie. I'm deeply and passionately and irrevocably in love with you."

His lips suddenly twisted. She couldn't take her eyes off them.

"I was afraid I had a big red sign painted on my forehead for all to see, but I couldn't help it." He caressed her with his eyes. "I didn't want to help it."

He pulled her to him, and she lost herself in his arms.

When he turned her loose, she murmured, "But I lied to you, Brett. How can you love me when I did such a horrible thing?"

He chuckled, a soft, delightful sound. "You didn't have to *be* married in order to get the job," he said, a laugh in his voice. "You only had to *say* you were married. As long as the hands considered you off limits, then everything was under control." He kissed her gently and said, "That makes me just as much a part of your deception as you were. I knew about the lie, but I let it stand."

She closed her eyes and let out a pain-filled sigh. "How can I go back? This is going to make so much trouble."

"Didn't you hear me?" he asked. "I love you, Katie. Will you marry me?"

She threw her arms around him. "Yes! I will!" Tears seeped out between her closed eyelids. "I've never wanted anything so much in my life."

They moved to the sofa to cuddle and whisper and ask the questions that all lovers ask: When did you know? What did you think of me when we first met? And a hundred more.

"When we lost our cattle, I started doubting God," Katie said. "I wondered where He was when the food ran low and we didn't hear from Pa. I couldn't understand why He'd allowed so much misery to come to us." She paused, gazing into the center of the room, forming her words. "I couldn't feel Him," she looked at Brett, "but He was always there."

"He led you to me," Brett told her. "There's no way I can properly thank Him for that."

Awhile later he got up to stoke the fires, then returned to her side. They talked of the future and marveled over the past.

When the thirty-day clock struck four times, Katie let out a sleepy giggle. "It's time to start breakfast. I'd best put on the coffeepot."

"This early on Christmas morning?" he asked.

"Especially on Christmas morning," she retorted. "Those kids will be down here in full force thirty minutes from now. After that no one will sleep, believe me."

He pulled her close for one last kiss. "Before you do that, there's something I have to ask you," he said.

"What?"

"I have this rule about no single women on my ranch," he drawled. "I can't change that now."

"Does that mean I'm out of a job?" she asked.

"Quite the contrary," he said with a grin. "It only means we'll have to travel to Pueblo when we leave here. Before we go back home, I've got to find a parson to make an honest woman of you!"

Epilogue

The Masten Ranch
May 24, 1885

Dear Pa and Ma,

Thanks so much for your last letter. I'm always thrilled to hear from you. I was glad to learn that Albie and Jane are safely at home with their father. Pa, please send directions to their ranch so Brett and I can visit them after the baby is born.

I've spent the last three days sewing curtains out of blue calico. Duffy has been hanging them up for me. Next project, we're going to move Brett's desk into a corner of the sitting room so we can make a nursery out of his office. He never uses that room anyway.

News flash. Rollie Barker is dating a girl from Rosita. She's the mayor's daughter, and he's got it bad. The hands are ribbing him from morning to night. He's the biggest tease around, so I have to laugh at him getting his payback.

I miss you all. I can't wait for you to come in the fall.

Love,
Katie

Dear Reader,

Although I was raised in an Amish/ Mennonite family, my parents divorced when I was thirteen. Deeply wounded by an abusive stepfather, I was extremely shy. Through a series of very painful events, I was cut off from my parents for five years. As God healed my wounded heart, my true personality slowly unfolded. Now I love talking to people, making new friends, and sharing my faith.

I had been a writer for years, but had never sold a novel. During this healing time, my books began to be published. My first novel, *Megan's Choice,* was a reader's favorite, and I was a favorite new author with Heartsong Presents. *Fireside Christmas* received four stars from *Romantic Times* and appeared on the CBA best-seller list for three months. Then my historical mystery, *Reaping the Whirlwind,* won the coveted Christy Award in 2001. My last release, *Colorado,* has sold more than 167,000 copies to date. To God be the glory. Great things He hath done.

Because I spent so many years struggling as a beginning writer, I have a heart to help people who have plenty of talent but who need personal guidance to cross the hurdle into publishing. In 2006 I founded Christian FictionMentors.com, a twelve-lesson interactive program that guides new writers through their first novel.

My husband, David, and I were missionaries on the tiny island of Grenada, West Indies, from 1987 to 2001 with our seven children. While there, I wrote *Survival Cookbook: For Americans Abroad,* 250 recipes for cooking-challenged Americans who can no longer purchase convenience foods. The cookbook is now in its third printing.

I never dreamed that one day I'd love speaking and even appear on radio and television. God continues to broaden my horizons, and I can't thank Him enough.

Visit www.askroseydow.com to ask me any question you may have regarding the writing life, any future books on my horizon, from-scratch cooking questions, or anything at all. You'll see a date there for my next live interview by teleconference. Or visit my Web site at www.roseydow.com. See you there!